Iron Pipeline

The Stopper Files, Volume 1

Eugene Lloyd MacRae

Published by CreateSpace, 2017.

IRON PIPELINE

First edition. June 9, 2017.

Written by Eugene Lloyd MacRae.

Chapter 1

OTTAWA, CANADA

MERLIN ARTHUR DRAGON had always felt uncomfortable with new situations. No, make that uncomfortable with the *people* he met in new situations. And that was how he felt as he stepped inside Interpol's National Central Bureau office for Canada to meet with Director Aubrey Laurent.

The only problem was...there was no office. All Merlin saw was two thousand square feet of empty space. His footsteps echoed lightly off the walls as he wondered if there was a door leading to another space that *was* occupied. A slight sound to his left caught his attention and he realized there was someone sitting behind a battered old desk inside an office that was devoid of anything else. Merlin moved across the floor to the open doorway and knocked on the frame before stepping inside.

A bear of a man with curly white hair and a fluffy white beard looked up from behind the oak desk and barked, "Yeah?"

"Director Aubrey Laurent?"

"Who wants to know?"

"I was told to report to you today, sir. Merlin Dragon?"

"Who?"

"Merlin–"

"I heard you the first time. Welcome to your first day at Interpol."

"Thank you–"

"Now forget you're in Interpol. No one can know."

Merlin blinked at the comment, "I wasn't aware we hid our attachment to Interpol–"

"The others don't. You will, Mr. Dragon. And you are not attached to Interpol as a member of the RCMP. You are now an Interpol agent, lock, stock and barrel. All the paperwork has been completed."

"It has?"

"Didn't I just say that?" Laurent pulled open a lower drawer on the right side of his desk. He reached in and pulled out a thick envelope, dumping the contents on the desk and tossing the envelope back in the drawer, "That's your Interpol badge, credentials, cell phone, 999 key–"

Merlin placed two fingers on the object, "A...999 key?"

"Yeah. It's used to break and enter. Do you know how to pick a lock?"

"No–"

"Learn. That thing is also called a bump key. It can open 90% of all cylindrical locks. You stick it in a lock and tap the end with something to drive it in. It might take a few taps but you'll eventually spring the lock and you're in." Laurent leaned forward and pushed another item toward Merlin, "And *that* is your special passport."

Merlin reached down, hesitated as his fingers wrapped around the passport and then he picked it up. Opening the cover, he looked inside, "What do you mean by special...?"

Laurent sat back, placing his hands on the chair's arms. He began rocking lightly as he watched Merlin closely, "Because it's tied into the government offices of all 190 countries who are a part of Interpol. You, Mr. Dragon, will be free to move freely across virtually every border in the world."

Merlin's brow furrowed as he closed the passport, "I wasn't aware Interpol could do that."

"The others can't, only *you* can...as you track down criminals."

Shaking his head, Merlin said, "I wasn't aware Interpol made arrests on sovereign soil around the world–"

"Interpol doesn't. And you're not *expected* to make arrests either. Do you have a weapon on you?"

Merlin felt totally confused, "No, sir. I know Interpol agents don't carry guns–"

"The others don't. You will." Laurent reached back into the drawer and pulled out a conceal holster holding a handgun. He set it down with a thud on the desktop, "This is a special, 9mm, carbon fiber Beretta PX4 Storm Subcompact handgun. It can pass through metal detectors without a problem and it has Smart Gun technology. The grip has an internal scan of your palm print and can't be fired by anyone else."

"It has *my* palm print already. How–?"

"How do you think? You work for me now. *All* of your files are now in my possession."

Merlin heard the leather slide over the oak desk as Laurent pushed it toward him, "I see...."

"From this day on, you carry a weapon, Mr. Dragon. What you do with it is up to you."

Shaking his head, Merlin said, "I'm sorry, Director Laurent, but I don't understand–"

"It's very simple. The member countries like the United States, Great Britain, Canada, France, Germany, Italy–" Chester waved a hand in the air, "And on and on and on. It doesn't matter. What they have decided is that we need a new method to deal with an increasing number of bad players around the world. Specifically, the *worst* of the bad players. *You* are that method."

"Me?"

"Didn't I just say that?"

Merlin opened his mouth and then closed it.

"We chose *you* because you have a high moral compass, Mr. Dragon. Your psychological tests indicate you are a man who will do the right thing. Always. If that means using that weapon...." Laurent rocked gently, gauging Merlin's reactions before he spoke again, "The people we send you after will be a danger to a member country for any number of reasons. They may even be a threat to the entire world. But whatever the reason, all of your assignments will be threats we can't deal with effectively through the federal, state or local police forces of a member country. And these threats will have to be dealt with quickly. They will need to be stopped dead. That's where you come in."

"Me?"

"Didn't I just say that? *You* are The Stopper, Mr. Dragon. Do you understand?"

Merlin's fingers rested on the leather holster as he considered the words. A moment later he said in a low voice, "Yes, sir. I understand."

"If you decide you don't want to do the job, you will be taken from here to a lonely spot in the woods and *shot*."

His eyes flicking up at the comment, Merlin watched Laurent's chest for movement as his fingers began to move toward the weapon's trigger in the holster.

Laurent gave him a mischievous grin, "Just screwing with you." The grin disappeared, "That tells me you won't hesitate to do what has to be done. Despite the fact you've been a paper pusher for five years with the Canadian Army and the last four years with the Royal Canadian Mounted Police, you have natural instincts for this job. Your talents were being wasted."

Merlin's eyes dropped back to the gun and a moment later he drew his fingers away. There was a definite feeling of surprise in the pit of his stomach.

Laurent gestured to the cell phone on the desk, "Anybody who picks up your phone and looks at it will see a few generic apps and little else. It's not even set up to ask for a password or a PIN number."

Merlin's attention went to the phone and he picked it up, "So it's just a generic phone?"

"Hardly. That cell phone is already set up with a profile of your facial features."

"How–? Never mind."

A Cheshire-cat grin split Laurent's face, "It has advanced facial recognition software and will know it's you automatically. When *you* look at it, the special features will be unlocked."

"Special features?

"Your cell phone is connected to Interpol's I-24/7, our secure global police network. As the name implies, you can access our databases 24 hours a day, 365 days a year. All 190 member countries of Interpol add their information on a constant basis to our databases. You'll be able to search and cross-check information on just about anything in a matter of seconds. Criminals profiles, stolen and lost travel documents or administrative documents, stolen motor vehicles, fingerprints, DNA profiles, stolen works of art, whatever you need."

Raising an eyebrow, Merlin turned the phone on, "It's an Internet connection?"

"Or satellite. Whatever it needs to connect you. It will automatically roll through the connections available to it, breaking passwords as necessary without you needing to do a single thing. All your messages and calls will be one hundred percent secure. You can also contact me but try to keep that to a minimum. I don't want to be in the middle of a wine party and have you interrupting me."

His brow furrowed as Merlin considered Laurent's comment.

A moment later, Laurent winked at him.

Merlin straightened up, letting his breath out slowly as he considered the items on the desk.

Director Aubrey Laurent's chair rocked gently again, his voice low, "In this job, you're not chained to a desk, performing tasks that are important, but ones that can leave you frustrated at the end of the day. And from here on, Mr. Dragon, you make all the decisions. Out there in the field, you decide what needs to be done. And you work *alone.*"

That last fact was definitely appealing to Merlin. He certainly wasn't–

Laurent's voice grew deadly serious, "There are a lot of bad actors out there, Mr. Dragon. In your last four years of pushing paper with the RCMP, you've seen some of them. And you've felt the same sting of frustration we all feel when we see the limitations our regular law enforcement methods have on putting a stop to them. Like I said before, there are bad actors out there that even threaten the very fabric of our world. *You* can move beyond the sting of frustration, beyond the limitations. *You* have the opportunity to do whatever it takes to remove those threats."

There was a silence in the room as Merlin considered the words. The task was both intriguing and daunting.

And then, out in the empty office space, a female voice called out, "Hello?"

Merlin turned to see a woman with silver hair and a bright smile standing ten feet or so outside the office.

Laurent stood up, "That's Evelyn." As he walked around the desk, he gave Merlin a serious look, "And you never saw her, get it?"

Merlin nodded, "Got it."

Another mischievous grin lit up Laurent's lips, "Evelyn is my lady friend. She works for Interpol–"

"I'm not your lady friend," Evelyn chided him as he stepped out of the office, "I'm your girlfriend."

"It sounds too permanent," Laurent complained. He glanced back at Merlin and winked. Then he greeted the woman warmly with a hug.

Merlin stood in the doorway, wondering if he should shake hands with Evelyn or–

Laurent draped an arm around her shoulder and his countenance turned serious again as he looked Merlin in the eyes, "There's an armored limousine waiting for you outside, Mr. Dragon. It will pick you up for every assignment and take you to a private area at the airport where a plane is on constant stand-by, ready to fly at a moment's notice. That's where you're going right now. I'm sending you on your first assignment. It's an easy one, just to get you started. You will receive your instructions after take-off. Don't keep the plane waiting, Mr. Dragon. If you do...keep the woods in mind."

Laurent then turned Evelyn around and walked with her toward the exit, discussing plans for lunch.

Chapter 2

MERLIN DRAGON DID keep the plane waiting. He had something important to do first. As soon as he stepped into his third-floor, Stonecliffe Arms apartment, Jigs bounded away from his usual spot on the built-in window perch and padded across the floor. Merlin opened his arms and the blue, wooly Chartreux cat leaped into them and began purring. Merlin had found him while in pursuit of a thief who had knocked an elderly woman down and stolen her purse. Chasing the thief into an alleyway, Merlin had slipped on wet cardboard and landed hard on his back. Looking up, he saw a kitten sitting on a garbage can looking down at him with a look that was half curiosity and half amusement. He never caught the thief but he made a friend for life.

Merlin scratched Jigs' head, "Sorry, pal but I have to take a trip. But I think you're going to enjoy yourself."

Jigs nudged Merlins's face and flashed one of his brilliant Chartreux smiles.

"Oh, You're already anticipating the chicken bits you sneak from her plate are you? And yes, I know about them." Merlin went back into the hallway and down three apartments where he knocked softly on Jaimee Hartman's door. A willowy beauty with jet black hair and a bubbly personality, Hartman had moved into

9

the building a year ago. Jigs had taken a liking to her the first day they met in the lobby. Jaimee was a professional graphic designer working for a major media corporation and since most of her work was done on a computer, she mainly worked from home, sending files back and forth over the Internet. When she found out Merlin boarded Jigs with a local veterinarian when he was away for work, she volunteered to babysit Jigs and the cat loved the arrangement

It took a moment before the door swung open and the scent of peppermint tea and woody potpourri gently washed over Merlin.

Jaimee's bright blue eyes lit up, "Hi, Merlin."

Merlin was never good with women and he had always wondered if the fact her eyes lit up when she saw him was her natural manner with people or if she was interested in him specifically. Despite wanting to ask her out, he had always chickened out on the reasoning that he might be wrong and he would feel foolish if he was rejected and—

"Is there something I can do for you?"

That snapped Merlin from his thoughts and he felt his face flush slightly. Especially when he saw her eyes sparkle. She either knew exactly what he was thinking or— Merlin cut off his own rambling thoughts, "Uh. Yeah. Hi, Jaimee. I have a favor to ask."

"You want to sleep over?"

Merlin felt his mouth open and then close.

"Just kidding." Jaimee reached for Jigs, "Hey, buddy. I guess it's you and me again for a few days."

Jigs didn't wait to be asked twice and he snuggled into her arms.

She rubbed Jigs on the head, "Or will you be gone for longer, Merlin?"

Merlin scratched his head, Uh, I'm not sure. I've...." Laurent's words came back to him. 'Forget you're in Interpol. No one can know.' Not sure how to put it, Merlin finally said, "I've been transferred to a position in the government and–"

"You're not with the Mounties anymore?"

"Uh...yes, but...."

Jaimee put a hand up, "No problem. I've lived in this town long enough, And my cousin works for the government, so I know there are things people can't talk about. It's perfectly fine."

"Thanks. I appreciate your understanding. And I'm sorry to put you out like this."

Waving his concerns away, Jaimee said, "You're not putting me out. Me and Jigs here love our time together." She massaged the cat on the head, "Isn't that right, Jiggsy?"

Jigs cuddled and smiled.

Merlin nodded, "Thanks, Jaimee." He turned to leave and then turned back, digging into a pocket and pulling out several folded twenty dollar bills. He held them out to her, "I almost forgot. Spend whatever you need to and I'll reimburse you for anything extra."

Jaimee took the cash in hand and gave Merlin an innocent look, "Can I get myself one of those male strippers that does house calls?"

Merlin's eyebrows knit together, "Pardon?"

"Never mind. Just joking." She shooed him away with a wave of her hand, "You just do what you have to do and you don't worry about Jigs. We'll be fine."

"All right. Thanks." Halfway down the hallway, he heard Jaimee call out softly, "Merlin? Keep in mind that sleeping over thing if you ever need to."

Merlin looked over his shoulder, heard a giggle and the closing of a door.

Chapter 3

THE AIRCRAFT WAITING for Merlin Dragon was a brand-new Bombardier Global 8000, an ultra-long-range business jet. There would normally be a crew of four and seventeen passenger seats. But on *this* jet, there was a crew of two. The pilot, Captain Charity Sherrell and the co-pilot, Captain Faith Saab, were both members of the Canadian military and greeted him officiously. And Merlin was the only passenger. He was informed again this was *his* jet, on-call for whatever assignment he was given. The main cabin area on this jet contained just four plush seats, two of them with a table. The area in front of them contained a long sofa, a television and a mini-bar. Captain Saab informed him there was a galley just through the doorway toward the back that was fully stocked if he needed a meal or just a coffee. Beyond that was a suite with two single beds, a private washroom, and a true stand-up shower.

Sherrell and Saab disappeared into the flight cabin and Merlin was barely seated when the TechX high bypass turbofan engines came to life in a deep, buzz-saw moan. The feeling of immense power surged through the cabin.

Twenty minutes after a smooth take-off, Merlin's cell phone buzzed. A secure text message told him he would find details of his assignment in a secure locker in the suite. The message held the code for the electronic lock. He retrieved a thick envelope and a backpack and he sat in one of the plush chairs, setting them on the table.

He first turned his attention to the envelope entitled Iron Pipeline; Case #65380. He slid out a large number of files and reports onto the table and he flipped through the pages. Apparently, the term Iron Pipeline was referring to Interstate Highway 95, the route that runs from Florida to New England. It was being used to smuggle guns from states with looser gun restrictions to the ones that were tighter. New Jersey and New York were the main targets for this arms trafficking and you could get five to ten times what you paid for a weapon, depending on what you were selling. Florida, Georgia, North Carolina and Texas were the southern feeder states. But Arizona, California, Indiana, Ohio, Pennsylvania, and Virginia were also part of the ten-state block where half the interstate-trafficked guns recovered at crime scenes came from. Some weapons were picked up at gun shows through private sales, where few questions were asked. But many came from a constant break and enter rampage on gun shops. The more gun shops a state had, the more likely they would be a feeder state of weapons getting into the hands of felons.

Merlin shook his head. How was he supposed to stop all that? Then he realized he was supposed to focus on a specific militia group who were working from the area around Gainesville, Georgia. They called themselves the Coal Mountain Militia. The city of Atlanta, only 55 miles away from them, was a major hub for gun running and the group was suspected of hitting gun shops there constantly to get firearms to sell on the black market. It didn't make much sense to Merlin to just focus on one single group like this and then Laurent's words came back to him; 'It's an easy one, just to get you started.' The hard stuff would no doubt come later. If he proved himself.

Laying the paperwork on the table, Merlin turned his attention to the backpack. Unzipping it, he pulled everything out.

There was a brown plaid shirt, a denim jacket, blue jeans with a belt and a pair of leather boots with laces. Why would they give him an outfit like this? Probably to fit in– no, that was only partly true. It was the boots that gave him a clue. Or should he say, the shoelaces. Because the ends of the shoelaces on each boot had blacked-brass tips and he knew exactly what they were from his days in the army. One tip on each lace was actually a boot-lace handcuff key. The design had been created for covert units of the U.S army that had a high possibility of being captured by the enemy.

The shirt was ordinary as were the blue jeans and the denim jacket. Nothing unusual there.

He checked the belt. It was made of 1.5" nylon webbing, completely non-metallic and he had seen one like it before. It was part of the kit for some of Canada's elite forces. It looked ordinary but had some features that were definitely *not* ordinary. The inside of the belt buckle itself held a non-metallic handcuff key and a ceramic razor blade. The inside of the belt webbing had dozens of elasticized compartments, ideal for stashing currency or other small items. This one had three items already loaded. Another non-metallic handcuff key, 4.5 feet of Kevlar survival cord and one item, an American Liberty nickel that was confusing at first, He turned it over several times and then remembered hearing about it. Turning the nickel to heads-up, he slid a fingernail clockwise along the edge – there it was – a small blade of hardened stainless steel rotated out. He put the blade back in and then slipped the 'coin' into his back pocket. If someone searched him, it was doubtful they would worry about a coin in his back pocket. But if he had his hands tied behind his back by zip ties or duct tape, he could use this to escape. The thought was sobering, though. If they were giving him escape tools, they must expect he would need them sooner or later.

ATHENS-BEN EPPS AIRPORT, Athens, Georgia

The landing was smooth and as they rolled to a stop, Merlin saw a Georgia State trooper on the black tarmac standing next to a red pickup truck. Another plain vehicle was behind the pickup, a trooper sitting behind the wheel. Merlin assumed the truck was his transportation and he shook his head as he headed for the exit. He was now wearing the plaid shirt under the denim jacket, the blue jeans complete with special belt and lastly the boots. Inside that red pickup, he would either fit in or stick out like the proverbial sore thumb.

The weapon he had been given was now in a concealed carry holster in the waistband of his jeans over his back right pocket and the cell phone was in a holder on his hip.

As Merlin stepped out onto the top step of the airstairs built into the aircraft, he wondered if he should have brought along the Interpol badge and the passport to show the trooper. He knew undercover officers often carried both their badge and their police identification card but he had no idea if he did that as an Interpol agent. Especially with Laurent's words; 'Now forget you're in Interpol. No one can know.' But once on the tarmac, as he approached the heavy-set trooper, the man simply gave him a nod and stuck his hand out, "I'm Colonel Watts, sir."

Merlin wasn't really sure how he should greet the trooper and he simply gave back a nod of acknowledgment, playing it out by ear.

Watts gestured to the red pickup, "This is used by our under-cover team. It's clean as a whistle and registered under the name of Caleb Rucker. There's a driver's license in the glove box under that name with your picture. The boys did a great job getting it done on the short notice your people gave us. The address is a rooming house in Atlanta. Our Georgia law says you have 60 days to change your address so you can use that tidbit of information to divert any-one checking on it. There's also a bank card under that same name that you can use to get cash from ATM machines. Your people are footing that bill."

Merlin nodded in acknowledgment.

Watts gestured to a gate in the distance behind the jet, "You come and go through gate number 19 down there. That's used by the police down here and the guards at the gate have your picture and your prints. They'll scan you on the way back in." Then the trooper simply touched the brim of his stetson in salute, "Good luck on whatever you're here for." He turned on his heels and head-ed to the car behind the pickup. A moment later, the car was tear-ing away across the tarmac.

Merlin stood watching and then heard a voice behind him. He turned to see the pilot, a young woman with short dark hair, stand-ing at the top of the airstairs. It took a moment and then the name came to him, it was Captain Sherrell.

"We'll be right here waiting for you, sir, " Sherrell said. She jerked a thumb back over her shoulder, "Me and Saab will take turns crashing on a bed and watching for you, no matter how long it takes And if you come across any of that Georgia corn moon-shine with the big, black Xs we heard about, keep us in mind." With that said, she turned and headed back into the aircraft, leaving Merlin standing by himself on the tarmac.

Merlin felt all alone and he looked up into the sky. The day was warm and humid and he could see cumulonimbus clouds forming in the distance. He wondered if that was an omen. Would he be gathering his own storm clouds before long?" He would find out soon enough. Heading to the red pickup, he found it unlocked and the keys in the ignition. And just as the trooper had said, he found a driver's license in the glove box and he repeated the name; Caleb Rucker. There was also a paper that was wrapped around something. That something turned out to be the bank card. The PIN number was printed on the paper. He memorized it, ripped up the paper and stuck the pieces in one of the cup holders. He would burn it later.

The pickup didn't have a navigation system so he checked his cell phone. Sure enough, it had a GPS app and he called it up, asking for the route from here to Gainesville. He set everything in place and was now only forty-four miles away from his first assignment.

Taking a deep breath and letting it out in a sharp exhale, he nodded to himself and stuck the license and bank card in his jacket pocket, "Okay, Caleb, let's go see how easy this easy case is. And try not to get killed doing it."

Chapter 4

GAINESVILLE, GEORGIA

THE COUNTY SEAT of Hall county, the city of Gainesville (also known as the Queen City of the Mountains) is on the southern edge of the Blue Ridge Mountains and nestled against Lake Lanier, making it the tourism and economic center of Northeast Georgia. And Merlin was happy to see the city teeming with out of state license plates. He would easily fit in with a lot of tourists not knowing their way around. He found the road he needed that would take him to the northwest part of the city and thirty minutes later he found himself pulling off the road across from the Chattahoochee Roadhouse.

It was getting late and gaudy lights lit the place up like a firecracker. Even from here he could hear the country and western music blasting across the full parking lot. This was the spot where he was supposed to try and make some type of contact with the Coal Mountain Militia.

Then a thought struck Merlin. He'd come all this way and now sat across from the roadhouse without a plan. Yeah, right, just walk in there and ask them to 'take me to your leader', just like some alien from outer space. He sat miffed at himself, trying to figure out a plan.

How about asking if he could buy some guns nearby? No, he'd have to pretend he was an ex-con and he had no background story in place so they could check him out. And then he'd have to explain why he just happened to pick this town and this specific roadhouse. And since he only had one gun, he couldn't try and offer a load of weapons to someone because then he'd have to go steal some. He shook his head. This business was turning out harder than he thought. How was he supposed to do this?

He decided to play it by ear. All he could do was go inside and give it a once over. Maybe something would come to him. He put the red pickup in gear and crossed over the road, angling into the parking lot and parking alongside a ton of other pickup trucks. At least his transportation would fit in. As he got out and closed his door, Merlin waited a moment to slip in behind two couples who had driven into the lot just after he did. As soon as they opened the entrance door, the pounding bass of the music rocketed into the stratosphere and vibrated through his skeleton. At least, that's how it felt to Merlin who was used to the lighter jazz music at the club not far from his apartment. As the door closed behind him, the powerful music and laughter embraced him in a bear hug while the aroma of pulled pork, BBQ chicken breasts and the scent of cold beer reminded him he hadn't eaten since breakfast. He pushed that aside for now and threaded his way through the crowd toward the bar. The long glass behind the dark oak counter reflected every kind of whiskey, bourbon, tequila, and vodka you could imagine. A series of tap handles indicated there was cold draft beer on tap as well. It didn't look like a place where you would order a drink with an umbrella and survive very long.

As he fit himself between two large men in heavy work clothes, Merlin bellied up to the bar and looked over the tap handles.

A burly bartender with long, slicked back hair, wiped the counter in front of him and leaned forward to be heard over the music and buzz of conversation, "Yes, sir. What can I get for you?"

"I'm just looking to see what kind of draft you have–?"

The burly man shot a thumb over his shoulder, "We got a draft we brew right here on the premises. Can't get no better."

"All right. That'll do."

The bartender stepped two tap handles over, grabbed a mug and poured a stream of pale golden liquid.

Merlin set a twenty on the counter and the bartender thumped the mug down on the counter before grabbing the bill and turning around to a cash register. A thick foam slid over the edge of the mug as Merlin picked it up. He took a quick drink of the cold beer and he had to agree it tasted good. Wiping foam from his lips, he turned and looked across the room. A number of couples were dancing on a large area of the floor off to the left and he watched them move to the beat of some country song he vaguely remembered hearing on the radio. A table full of men and women on the edge of the dance floor clinked glasses and lifted their mugs high in some raucous salute. The clink of change on the counter behind him caught his attention and Merlin turned to thank the bartender and offer a tip. But the burly man was already down the bar and grabbing another mug for a customer. Turning to face the noisy crowd again, Merlin leaned back against the bar, trying to look as casual as possible as he sipped on the beer.

A tall, audacious redhead, working her way through the crowd, looked directly at him and then raised an eyebrow, giving his body the once-over.

Merlin, at 5-10 and 175 lbs, with brown hair and green eyes, had never been called handsome or a stud and he felt immensely flattered.

The redhead walked a few more steps toward the dance floor as she continued to eye Merlin and then she slowed her pace, turning her head to a husky, greasy haired man behind her. She said something to him and then she made a slight gesture with her head toward Merlin before continuing on.

Greasy-haired man on the other hand, stopped and glared menacingly toward Merlin. Then he turned and said something to a couple of other rough looking men. The two men shot menacing grins across the floor at Merlin and then gestured for the women they were with to follow the redhead.

When Merlin looked back at greasy-haired man, he was only a few feet away and leaning his body forward, his voice a growl through the loud music.

"You trying to be funny by trying to pick up my woman there, pal?"

Merlin wasn't sure what he was talking about and shook his head, "I'm not sure–"

Greasy-haired man shot a thumb over his shoulder, "You calling Morgan a liar? She told me the gesture you made to her."

Glancing across the floor, Merlin saw the redhead watching the whole thing, a half-smile on her lips. He looked back, "I'm sorry, but–" A fist was already on its way. Instinctively, Merlin leaned his head to the right, letting the fist sail past. Then he swung his own right hand with the beer hard back across his body, smashing it into his attacker's head. Beer, foam, and glass exploded everywhere.

Greasy-haired man was on his way to the floor when the other two men attacked.

Merlin brought his left hand up and threw a stiff-fingered blow into the first man's throat.

The man staggered back, gagging and holding his throat.

Merlin felt rather than saw a blow coming from man number three and he angled his head and body to the left.

Most of the force from man number three's right cross was deflected by the rolling of Merlin's head and he swore. He lowered his shoulder and drove into Merlin, continuing his attack.

Driven hard back against the bar, Merlin grunted, lifted his arms, clasped his hands overhead and brought them down hard onto the man's lower back.

The man groaned in agony from the blow to his kidney area, collapsed to his knees and fell forward.

Stepping over the still falling body, Merlin looked for some open space to give himself a buffer before the three resumed their attack–

Several sets of hands grabbed him, lifted him off his feet and propelled him forward through the swiftly parting crowd.

"Throw them outta here!" yelled a voice from behind the bar.

There was a lot of cussing and whooping and hollering as Merlin moved toward the front exit without taking a single step on his own. The door was opened by a grinning woman and a heartbeat later, Merlin felt himself thrown forward and he rolled several times from the force before he came to rest on his back outside the roadhouse. A moment later, he heard the sounds of scuffling and the thump of three meat sacks hitting the ground behind him.

The loud music and raucous laughter from inside the roadhouse were muted as the door was slammed shut.

Merlin rolled over to his knees, ready to continue the fight.

But the three men were still on the ground where they had been tossed, groaning in agony. Greasy-haired man put a hand to the right side of his head where he was bleeding.

Deciding retreat was in order, Merlin got to his feet and backed away. He heard laughter behind him and he whirled.

Several men and women were heading toward him, and the roadhouse. Apparently, this was a common occurrence because they didn't look concerned at all. Instead, they were laughing and pointing at the three men still on the ground.

Skirting the laughing crowd, Merlin headed for his vehicle, digging for his keys. It took him a moment to finally find his red pickup and he quickly climbed inside, starting the engine. The tires screeched and spit out loose gravel as he slammed down on the gas and he was on the road and away from the roadhouse in the blink of an eye. Glancing in the rearview mirror, Merlin didn't see any signs of the men or anyone else following him. Merlin lightly pounded the side of his fist on the steering wheel. So much for being undercover and discrete.

Chapter 5

MERLIN STAYED OVER in a nearby motel, rose before sunup and sat down in the International House of Pancakes across the road to have breakfast. The rich scent of his coffee, hash browns, sunny-side-up eggs and stack of strawberry banana pancakes sat untouched as he chewed on a piece of richly buttered toast, trying to figure out what he should do next. Or should he say first, since his starting attempt in this business was an abject failure.

"Are the eggs all right there, honey-bun?"

Merlin looked up to see his motherly, gum-chewing and pencil-behind-the-ear waitress looking down at him with concern.

"Uh, yeah. I was just thinking." Merlin set the toast on his plate and picked up his fork.

She patted him on the shoulder, "You eat and think later, honey-bun. You don't make me come back, you hear?" She gave him a smile and moved on to another table.

Merlin had to smile as well as he watched her over-the-top gushy attitude wash over her next table of customers. She reminded him of his mother– Merlin's smile disappeared as another set of eyes locked with his. It was the tall, gorgeous redhead from last night. She was standing across the diner, had probably just come in, and she raised one eyebrow, like she did last night, as she considered him. Unlike last night, when she wore a blouse and slacks, today she was dressed in a black dress that would be described as business-like. Described that way but on this redhead, the dress promised there was more than business in your future. It was several inches above the knee, showing off a pair of shapely legs.

A moment later, she headed directly for him, weaving her way through the other tables, the hint of that audacious smile on her full lips. Pulling out a chair, she sat across from him, set a small purse on the table and pulled the chair in, "Fancy meeting you here."

Merlin scratched the back of his neck and then said, "I don't remember asking you to sit down–?"

"It doesn't matter. I'm here now." She set her elbows on the table and clasped her hands together, resting her chin on them, "I was impressed with how you handled yourself last night–"

"Why? Are you the local wrestling coach or something? Is that why you started that thing? Because you're looking for new recruits?"

Her green eyes glittered, "I've been known to do a little wrestling with the boys but no. I just like the way you look. And Gavin was getting a little boring. His idea of a date was to take me out and shoot guns." She shrugged her shoulders, "And then *you* go and win the prize last night and what do you do? You go home without it."

Before he could answer, the waitress appeared beside the table, "Good morning, Morgan." She looked at Merlin, "Do I add her to your bill there, honey-bun?"

Merlin opened his mouth–

"Oh, I won't be charging him, Rose. It will *all* be on the house."

The waitress looked at the redhead and then broke out in a grin. She patted Merlin on the shoulder, "I think you got a whole heap of trouble coming there, honey-bun."

As the waitress moved on, the redhead winked across the table at Merlin.

Setting his fork down, Merlin looked across at her for a moment, "Look. Morgan is it? Look, Morgan—"

"You haven't told me *your* name yet...honey-bun."

Merlin was about to explain why she had to leave him alone when he realized he had forgotten what his name was supposed to be. Crap. This undercover stuff is harder—

The redhead gave him a lopsided smile, "Cat got your tongue there, honey-bun? Or you just thinkin' about all the things we're gonna do?"

Reaching into his pocket. Merlin pulled out the driver's license and took a quick peek at it. Caleb Rucker. He shook his head softly at his own stupidity. Forgetting such an important part of his undercover identity like that could get him killed. But he also realized this gave him a way back into the roadhouse. He stretched across the table and set the driver's license down at her elbow, "That's so you know I'm not lying when I say I'm Caleb Rucker. I'm just an upstanding citizen of—"

"Oh, Caleb," she said as her eyes flicked down to the license and then back to him, "I don't care if you're standing up, lying down or kneeling down...when we do it. Just as long as we do it." She winked.

Merlin picked up his fork to hide his discomfort. He wasn't sure if it was her talk or his feeling like a poor agent, but it was there. He reminded himself that she was his opportunity to rectify his situation as he cut into his eggs and he would have to deal with it either way, "Grab yourself some breakfast. And then we can take it from there."

She smiled, "Sorry, honey-bun, but I gotta go to work." She turned her head and called out, "Rosie? Would you please get my large coffee and two of them delicious cinnamon raisin bagels heated and ready to go?"

Rose was at another table, writing down another order and all she did was nod once and say, "Already done and ready for you at the counter, Morgan. Just waiting for you to get done your flirting. And, yes, I put it on his bill."

A few of the other customers snickered, apparently familiar with Morgan one way or another.

Morgan looked back at Merlin, still smiling and she rapped her knuckles lightly on the table, "I'll meet you back here at seven and we can get a nice plate of something." She leaned forward, the smile turning into something more pouty and her eyes sparkled, "Then we can get to know each other. Real well." She winked, got up and headed across to get her order.

Merlin just sat there, watching the redhead walk away. He couldn't help himself and his eyes dropped to her shapely legs below the short skirt. A moment later, he looked up to see Rose looking at him, a smirk on her face.

She winked at him and went back to taking her order.

Letting out a small breath of air, Merlin felt a little foolish. He felt a little like a schoolboy who had been manipulated by one of the pretty girls. She had done the same thing last night. Well...actually she had manipulated everyone. Then he felt a *lot* foolish. Here he had this fantastic cell phone that he could use to find out anything about anyone and he had no idea what Morgan's last name was. Or where she worked. Wasn't he supposed to be finding things out? This secret agent stuff was hard.

Finishing his breakfast, Merlin left enough to pay the bill and give Rose a big tip. As he headed for the door, Rose came from the kitchen area, carrying a couple of plates piled high with breakfast for another set of customers.

Rose gave him a smile as she passed, "Thank you, sir. And you have a good day."

Merlin turned quickly and lowered his voice, "Does my...?" He made air quotes, "*Girl friend* have lunch here? She asked me to meet her but...."

Rose raised an eyebrow, "No. From what I know, she eats at a place by where she works."

Clearing his throat, Merlin tried to look sheepish.

Shaking her head, Rosie said, "Doesn't surprise me with that one. She's one of them court reporters at the Federal Court over on Spring Street. One of the other girls here, Olivia, she worked at some place over there and said she used to see her all the time. Don't remember the restaurant though and Olivia's not in until later."

"Oh. Okay, thanks."

Rose shook her head as she walked away, throwing back over her shoulder, "Good luck with one, honey-bun."

Stepping outside, Merlin felt a bit more confident that he could find things out. Of course, he had to make himself look like a fool to do it, but it was progress. Which was why he hadn't asked about the last name. No sense looking like a *total* fool.

Chapter 6

AS MERLIN CLIMBED into the pickup truck, he realized something. He needed some *practice* as a 'secret agent'. It was a dumb idea, but true. He drummed his fingers on the steering wheel as he gave it some thought. What he had to do was build a dossier of people who frequented the roadhouse. And the first person he could start with was Morgan. That could be his 'practice'. Maybe she would turn out to be a part of this militia group but he doubted it. The question was, how would he start? The problem was simple but difficult. He could go to the United States Courthouse & Federal Building and just *ask* someone about her, like her last name. But a stranger asking about one of the women in the courthouse could set off alarm bells. And he would need more information than that to do a proper search. Facial recognition might work but he would need to take a picture of her. He started the engine and put the vehicle in drive, deciding to just go there and see what he could do.

The Federal Building was a four story, gray-stone and marble building with two guards at each entrance, manning metal detectors. He left his special Beretta in the glove box so he wouldn't have to worry about getting it through. Even though he was told it was undetectable, he didn't want to take the chance. Then he grabbed the ball cap from the passenger seat. He didn't want Morgan to spot him because he didn't want to have to explain why he was here, so he had stopped at a sports shop not far away and bought a University of Florida Gators' ball cap with the iconic green alligator logo. He left his jacket behind, pulled the cap low over his eyes and got out. Not much of a disguise but it would have to do.

Getting inside the building was easy. What he would do now that he was inside would be the hard part. He walked along the hallways, his footsteps echoing off the marble walls as he checked each courtroom as discreetly as possible. He was nearly caught on the second floor though when he almost bumped into Morgan. She was walking toward him but fortunately she was too busy talking to another woman. Merlin turned on his heels, pulling the cap lower. A moment later, he glanced back to see them disappear into a courtroom, the door closing slowly behind them. Merlin took a few minutes to see if she was coming back out and then went over and peeked inside. He saw her sitting in a chair behind a small table near the judge's bench. On the table was a steno machine. She was getting ready along with the other clerks for some case that was about to begin.

"Are you coming in, sir?"

Merlin realized it was a guard just inside the door, He was leaning and looking directly at him. "Uh, I'm just checking to see if my friend is here yet."

"You're the first one in, sir."

"Yeah. I'll just wait out here for them." He pulled back, letting the door close. Scratching the back of his neck, Merlin walked slowly along the hallway. Now all he had to figure out was what to do next. There were several benches along the far wall for people to sit while waiting to testify or for their case to start and he sat down on one of them to think. Not far down the hallway were the wash-rooms. A set for the court staff and a set for the public. That gave Merlin an idea. He waited until the hallway was clear to test his theory. He checked the door to the women's washroom for the court staff and it looked like it would work. It was risky but he couldn't think of anything else right now.

It took him an hour to get what he needed and to return, this time wearing his jacket. Morgan was still inside the courtroom, sitting at her desk, typing into the steno machine. Moving down the hallway, he got a coffee from the vending machine and took up a spot on a bench near the women's staff washroom. When it was quiet, he quickly went to the door and used a moist wipe to clean the surface of the stainless-steel door push-plate. The plate was used to protect the door from wear and tear but also to keep the surface clean from grime and fingerprints. Now all he had to do was return to the bench and wait. He sipped the coffee, enjoying the aroma more than the taste.

He had to wipe the plate clean several times over the course of the next hour until he finally saw Morgan step out of the court-room and head for the washroom. The problem was she was with a raven-haired young woman. He had to hope for the best as he held his breath, kept the ball cap low and the coffee cup up near his face.

Morgan and the woman talked as they walked and he felt the elation when it was Morgan who placed her hand on the push plate and led the way inside.

Merlin saw two men in suits down the hall but they were facing away as they talked. He had his chance. Setting his coffee down on the bench, Merlin slipped his hand into one of the pockets on the jacket. He had picked up a jar of woman's face powder and a fluffy powder brush and he pulled the powdered brush from his pocket and walked quickly across to the washroom door, keeping an eye on the men. He had already applied light powder to the bush and he lightly twirled it down the plate, just as he had seen on criminal investigation shows. He was thrilled to see the hand print and fingerprints appear. Slipping the brush back into his pocket, he pulled the cell phone out and took three quick images. Wiping the plate with the inside of his sleeve, he headed down the hallway for the stairs to the exit.

As he walked past the two men, he saw them glance at him and then give his jacket the once-over before resuming their hushed conversation. As Merlin reached the stairs and moved down them quickly, he looked down and grimaced. Makeup powder was all over the outside of his jacket's pocket. He brushed it away discreetly and chided himself. A sloppy secret agent could get killed if he was in a foreign country. Good thing his 'practice' was taking place in the good ole U.S. of A.

Chapter 7

MERLIN WENT BACK to the IHOP for his own late lunch so he wouldn't run into Morgan. After a delicious omelet, he nursed himself through a number of coffees and several pieces of blueberry pie until his cell phone buzzed. Surprisingly, his makeshift fingerprint kit and the phone images had worked. Apparently, a couple of the prints had been smudged but the others were perfect and a hit had been made.

The first thing he called up was an image of the driver's license for Morgan Grace Walker. Age: 27. Height: 5-10. Weight: 135. Hair: Red. Eyes: Green. Residence: Regent Landing Apartments, 200 Regent Court, Apt. 1, Gainesville, GA. Swiping across the screen, he brought up more information on her. All her schooling had been in Gainesville; Gainesville High School and then the Gainesville Campus of the University of North Georgia. She had taken the courthouse job after graduation. Like most people today, Morgan Walker had a social media presence and he clicked on the links. There wasn't much and he scrolled through pictures on one of her web pages. A lot were selfies, several taken with other female friends of hers in several different settings. It looked like a number were taken on a Caribbean vacation and there were two of Morgan in a very skimpy bikini. She had a great body. Marlin shook his head. This was all nice, but it was like her life was an open book and he wondered if someone could take advantage of that fact. Like breaking into her apartment because she was away, taking and posting pictures– he stopped swiping for a moment. There was something about the last picture. He swiped back and looked closer. It was a picture of three couples, Morgan and two other women, each sitting with a man. And the man Morgan was sitting with was the one who had attacked Merlin last night at the roadhouse. He tapped on the picture and, sure enough, each person was labeled from left to right; Travis Clarke (blow to the throat), Chloe Green, Morgan Walker, Gavin Perry (greasy-haired man and first punch thrown), Tyler Barnes (blow to the lower back), Brianna Long. He didn't really recognize the other two pretty, dark-haired women or if they had been at the roadhouse but he had been too busy ducking punches to pay any attention to them. But the other three were definitely the three, greasy toughs.

Merlin selected the picture and forwarded it to Interpol, along with the three names labeled left to right, asking for any and all information on them–

"Well, don't you look all absorbed in your phone."

Looking up, Merlin realized it was Morgan Walker. She had changed into a denim blouse and blue jeans and was right there beside the table. He glanced at the clock across the room and realized it was 4 o'clock. He had assumed she would be working until–

Morgan set her purse on the table, took a step and leaned over, kissing him on the lips. When she broke the short kiss off, she looked into his eyes, a grin on her face, "Are you one of those text-a-holics, Caleb Rucker?"

"Uh...no." Merlin slipped the phone into the holder. He felt his face burn.

Morgan stepped back across to pull her chair out, a very pleased grin on her face, "Hey, if it's porn. I don't mind." She sat and leaned forward, "And if you just blushed at a little ole kiss, what's it going to be like going a whole lot further?"

Merlin shook his head and had to smile at his own reaction, "I guess I'm just not used to beautiful women showing that kind of attention to me in public."

"How about in private?"

Clearing his throat, Merlin was mercifully saved by Rose appearing at the table, "And how are my two love-birds tonight?"

Morgan looked up, "Hi, Rosie. I'm surprised you're still here."

"Double-shift. Olivia and the other new one, Sara, called in sick. Must be something going around. Now what can I get y'all? Coffee to start?"

"Coffee would be good," Morgan agreed. "And why don't you bring us both your famous southern-steak plate with the fries and onion rings?" She looked across at Merlin, "I guarantee you'll like it."

Merlin wasn't hungry but he didn't argue. He just gave her a nod, "Sounds good to me."

Rose nodded, a smirk on her face as she looked at Merlin, "Got you by the nose-ring already, huh?" She walked away with a light chuckle at her own humor.

At least, Merlin hoped, she wasn't laughing *at* him. "So, how was work today?" he asked Morgan.

She shrugged as she took her purse from the table and set it at her feet, "Same old, same old." Setting her forearms on the table, she leaned on them, "But what about you? Where do you work?"

Merlin felt himself blink. Once again he really wasn't ready for this undercover stuff. He had no back story. No–

"Wow. You look embarrassed about it." She lifted her arms and set her chin on her hands, her eyes twinkling, "You're not one of them male strippers, are you? Why don't you get up on the table and show us your act?"

Shaking his head, Merlin felt his own discomfort and used it, "No. I'm just not very good around women–"

"You already used that line and you're already at the point of getting my pants off, so tell me something else."

Merlin marveled at the sparkle in her eye and her ease with herself. But the hesitation had given him time to make something up. And a half-truth was easier than a full lie. "I'm not working right now. I just got out of the military and I have a small pension."

Morgan's eyes took on a more serious look, "Oh."

"I'm just spending some time traveling–"

"Did you serve over in Iraq or one of those places?"

He shook his head again, "I really don't want to talk about it if you don't mind."

Now it was Morgan's turn to look uncomfortable and she sat back, "Sorry, I didn't mean to pry about that. I had high school friends who went over and never came back."

"Sorry to hear that."

"No problem." He gave her a smile, "So...are we going to the Chattahoochee Roadhouse after?"

Morgan genuinely looked surprised, "You want to go back there? After what happened?" She shook her head, "No. We can head over to the Vice Lounge. They have some great music over there and we can dance until we drop." She winked, "And who knows what we'll be doing after we drop?"

Merlin gave her a smile but he didn't feel it inside. This was going in the wrong direction.

The scintillating aroma of the southern-steak, onion rings and fries announced Rose's arrival and she appeared with two heaping plates, setting them down on the table, "Here you go. Y'all enjoy."

Morgan asked Rose for something but Merlin wasn't really listening at this point. Even the mouth-watering, wood-fired meal didn't do anything for his appetite. It shut down as his brain worked overtime on a plan from here

Chapter 8

AS MERLIN PICKED away at his meal, the cell phone on his belt vibrated. He set his fork down and rose from his chair, "Excuse me. I'll be right back."

Morgan bit into an onion ring, "Everything okay?"

"I'm just going to use the washroom."

"In the middle of eating?"

He put a hand on her shoulder as he passed and repeated, "I'll be right back."

Morgan shrugged and went back to her meal.

Merlin moved through the tables and pushed the washroom door open. There was one other customer at one of the sinks, washing his hands. Merlin slipped into the far stall and sat with the toilet seat down, pulling out his cell phone to see what he had. A report from Interpol on the image and names he had sent them popped up. Scrolling through it, he saw he had more information on Morgan Walker, listing family members and the date she had gone through customs for a trip to Barbados. His belief the picture had been taken on a Caribbean vacation had been confirmed by the digital geotags. There was also background information on Travis Clarke, Chloe Green, Gavin Perry, Tyler Barnes and Brianna Long. It showed Morgan Walker had worked at the courthouse for several years, and that Chloe Green had been working in a law office since leaving school, but it didn't show *any* employment for the men. Not one of them held down a job. And there was no indication when they had last worked. Merlin found that strange but he moved on to the rest of it.

All of them had grown up, gone to school and lived in the Gainesville area— no, take that back. Although she worked at the Gainesville Municipal Court, Brianna Long was actually from Coal Mountain, about thirty-six miles to the west of Gainesville. Shifting on the seat, Merlin wondered if he was better off trying to get close to this Brianna. It made sense.

Merlin headed back to the table, his mind whirling through different plans. He decided to use the simplest excuse. As soon as he got beside the table, he slipped a hand into his pocket, pulled out money and set it on the table to pay the bill.

Morgan looked at the bills, wondering what he was doing as she chewed on a French fry

He set a hand on Morgan's shoulder again, "I'm sorry. I think I'm coming down with something and I'm not feeling very good. I think I'll call it an early night and get some rest."

Morgan reached for her napkin as she swallowed quickly. She wiped her lips and was about to say something.

But Merlin didn't give her a chance, "I'll call you or drop by your apartment when I feel better. It's on Regent Court. Right?"

Morgan blinked a couple of times.

Walking away, Merlin heard her chair slide on the floor as she turned, confused by the sudden turn of events.

Rose stood near another table with a pot of coffee in one hand. She set the other hand on her hip as she watched Merlin pass her and head for the front door. A moment later, she glanced over at Morgan with curiosity.

Getting into the pickup, Merlin quickly started it and got going out of the parking lot, positive Morgan was going to be coming out to see him about what was going on. To his relief, or maybe disappointment, he didn't see her in his rearview mirror as he left the IHOP behind. He grabbed a coffee at a drive through and headed for the Chattahoochee Roadhouse. Backing the truck into a spot where he could watch the entrance as well as get a good look at most vehicles coming in, he turned off the engine and sat back.

As night fell, the lights of the Roadhouse exploded into a vibrant display of excitement and the country and western music rose in volume.

Merlin could feel slight vibrations through the body of the truck as the music reverberated across the parking lot. An hour passed and more and more people arrived, the laughter and chatter a constant undertone to the party atmosphere.

A black, Ford F-250 Super Duty pickup rolled into the parking lot and turned his way. As it passed, the dark figure driving was looking the other way and he couldn't see who it was. The Ford was parked in the shadows off to the left and a moment later a woman dressed in a loud, red dress walked away from the back of the truck toward the roadhouse. She had good legs–

Another vehicle pulled off the road. It was a blue Ford Explorer and it slowed to a stop for a moment.

Merlin saw the dark figure in the truck look his way. Crap. He set his cold coffee into a cup holder and pulled back a bit to stay in the shadows of the truck. Was that Morgan? If she had seen him.... No, he caught the profile of the driver. It was a woman but it wasn't

Morgan. He watched as she looked for a parking spot in the crowded lot. Was that Brianna Long?

The Explorer turned now to pass in front of him and he leaned forward. It sure looked like the same dark haired woman who had been with Morgan.

The woman parked the Explorer off to the left, four spots away from the black, Ford F-250 Super Duty pickup. She turned her lights off.

Merlin caught movement from the corner of his eye near the black pickup. A man with sandy hair and wearing dark clothing appeared near the back on this side and walked toward the Explorer. Merlin chastised himself. He had been so busy looking at that woman's legs he had failed to– something else caught Merlin's attention. It was the way the man scanned his surroundings as he walked. He was definitely wary of being seen for some reason.

The driver's door of the Explorer swung open and the woman got out. It *was* Brianna Long. She wore a blue blouse and blue jeans and held what looked like a thick, brown envelope. She walked to the back of her vehicle and met the man who leaned in and gave her a kiss. She passed the envelope to him, they talked for a minute and then she turned and extended her arm. The Explorer's lights flashed and the horn beeped twice as she locked the vehicle and then began walking toward the front entrance, saying something back over her shoulder.

Merlin saw the man watch Brianna Long walk away for a moment and then turn to his truck and bend over briefly before looking back at Long. He was checking to see if she...or anyone else...was looking. The man turned back to the truck and a glint of light gave Merlin the impression he had lowered the tailgate on his truck, then bent over again. It was too dark to see what he was doing, but whatever he was doing, it didn't matter right now. His staying at the truck gave Merlin his opportunity.

Turning his attention to the woman, Merlin slipped out of the truck. If he hurried, he might be able to 'accidentally' arrive at the front entrance the same time as she did. He really wasn't sure how he could start a conversation or catch her eye. Picking up women wasn't one of his skills and the possibility the man was her boyfriend and across the parking lot didn't make it any easier. But he had to try. This was 'the job'.

Pieces of gravel crunched under his boots as he jogged across the parking lot and the smell of BBQ ribs on the warm night air washed over Merlin as he reached the front entrance. He stood just off to the right of the door, hooking his thumbs over his belt and trying to look casual. His mind whirled as he tried to figure out exactly *how* he should get her attention.

Brianna Long was looking down as she walked but she looked up when she was only ten feet away and their eyes locked.

Merlin gave her a nod. Then he felt like an idiot when, for some reason, he stuck his hand out like a gun and said, "You're one of the ladies that was with Morgan last night."

The woman slowed her pace and then stopped and raised an eyebrow, "And you're that cowboy that started that fight." She crossed her arms over an ample chest, "Come back for more, did you?"

Shaking his head, Merlin said, "No, ma'am. But I sure am glad to see you."

Long gave him a dismissive look, "You hit on everything you see, cowboy?"

Merlin shook his head as well, giving her a smile, "No, just the pretty ones." It wasn't his best line, since he really didn't have any, but he was feeling good when he saw her eyes move down his body to his crotch.

She looked back into his eyes, a smirk on her face, "I know what you're thinking, cowboy. But you'll never get to use that on me."

His smile faded and Merlin felt like he was losing the situation. He had to get her to at least give him a chance, "No. It's not like that–"

"So now you're hitting on my girl?"

Merlin turned his head to see a man standing right there. It wasn't the man from the black pickup–

The name Tyler Barnes hit him at the same time as the sucker punch did.

Chapter 9

UNABLE TO ANTICIPATE the blow, it staggered Merlin. As he tried to bring his hands up to defend himself, his legs were kicked out from under him. He landed hard on his back and he felt and heard his breath expelled from his lungs with an audible whoosh. A blast of music washed over him as someone opened the entrance door and then it went back to the pounding, muted version. At first, he thought they had all gone inside, but no, there were now three sets of legs in blue jeans and heavy boots right there in front of him. His body jerked in pain as somebody kicked him from behind. That meant there were more than the three men he could see. The comments of an old army trainer came back to him: The best option when faced multiple opponents is not to fight them at all. Find some other way out of the situation. Yeah, he thought, good luck with that.

A voice in front of him said, "We're gonna make you look like you fell out of the ugly tree, boy."

As laughter sounded around him, Merlin's instincts kicked in before he knew it. He rolled over, trapping a pair of boots under his body and then punched the man in the crotch. As the yelp of pain sounded, Merlin was already rolling back and he spun around on the ground, taking out the legs of another man. Merlin was twisting his body for another attack by the time that man landed hard on his side and grunted in pain. Lifting his leg, Merlin slammed his foot into another man's knee. There was a cry of agony as he rolled for what he hoped was the last man.

He was. But the problem was the final man threw a boot at Merlin that struck him hard on the side of the head.

Stars whirled around Merlin's head from the blow but his body kept fighting. He fought the blackness that threatened to engulf him and he brought his legs around to try and take the last man down. He struck nothing but warm night air–

A heavy body landed on top of him. Legs straddled him. Hard blows rained down on Merlin's head.

Merlin heard more laughter and for some reason the body on top of him was suddenly gone. Before he could do anything else, Merlin felt his body picked up roughly by several sets of hands and he found himself carried away from the roadhouse. He grunted as his back hit the side of something hard. He felt a door handle against his back and realized he was against the door of a vehicle. Which meant he didn't have to worry about a rear attack. He brought his hands up–

A handgun was pointed straight at his face. The dark-haired man behind the gun stared intently into Merlin's eyes. His well-muscled arms rippled as if he wanted to pull the trigger. A moment later the man said, "You finished fighting, friend?"

Merlin slowly raised his hands in surrender and nodded slowly, "Yeah. I was just–"

"Stow it." The man's steel-gray eyes were hard. And then a moment later, amusement appeared, "You fight good, friend–"

"He's a son-of-a-bitch is what he is."

Moving just his eyes, Merlin saw Morgan standing next to the man, her eyes spitting fire.

"You dump me so you can go after Brianna?" she yelled.

Shaking his head just slightly so as to not make any sudden moves, Merlin said, "No. It's not like that–"

"Right. My eyes are playing tricks on me. You leave me at the diner, telling me you're feeling sick. And you end up here, hitting on my friend." She gestured behind her.

Merlin saw Brianna Long just behind Morgan, a look of amusement on her face. The sandy-haired man from the black pickup was standing beside her, his face impassive as he watched. Merlin glanced back at Morgan, let out a breath and just shrugged. He thought that would end it.

But Morgan moved closer, her voice rising in anger as she pointed an accusing finger at him, "And *how* is it that you know where I live? I never told you that."

Opening his mouth, Merlin started to reply but Morgan didn't give him a chance.

"Are you following me or something? Do you realize I know a lot of cops and judges and I could have you arrested–?"

The man with the gun held a hand up to her, "We don't need the cops. You go inside and I'll take care of it."

"But–"

"No buts. Do it. *Now*."

Morgan sneered at Merlin but backed away, joining Brianna Long and the men he had been fighting, now standing, holding sore spots on their body and glaring at him.

The man with the gun turned his head, "That means the rest of you, too."

There was a lot of grumbling and complaints of wanting revenge but they complied. The music blasted loudly, washing over everyone for a moment until they disappeared inside.

Merlin saw four other men still standing behind the man with the gun. They looked a lot harder and more dangerous than the men he had fought with tonight and last night.

There was a click as the handgun was cocked and moved closer to his face.

Chapter 10

MERLIN REACTED INSTINCTIVELY AGAIN, His right hand came up and slapped against the man's wrist as his left came up at the same tine and slapped against the gun, bending the wrist and taking the gun. In a heartbeat the situation was reversed, the gun in Merlin's hands and aimed at the man's face.

The dark-haired man froze in position.

The men behind him began reaching for weapons.

But the man held a hand out, knowing full well what they would do. A slow smile crept across his face, "It's okay, boys. Everything is cool." He gave Merlin a nod, "I'm impressed."

"Don't be," Merlin said, "I'd rather you be scared."

The smile stayed on the man's face, "Yeah. Well, good luck with that." He held his hands out, "Look. All I was doing was protecting friends. Now, if you'd like to move on, I would suggest you do that." He gestured to the side, "I'm sure someone will be calling the cops before long."

Merlin's eyes flickered to the side and behind the man, not wanting to take his eyes off him. There were a large number of people standing around, watching what was happening. A woman had her arms crossed but held a cell phone up and waggled it back and forth, sending a message to him. Either all these people were friends or acquaintances or just used to fights breaking out around the roadhouse. Merlin uncocked the gun, flipped it around and held it out, "No need for the cops. Let's just–"

The man took the gun and simply turned away as he slipped it into a holster under his shirt over his hip, "Let's go, guys."

Merlin was left standing there as the music blasted over everyone again as one of the other men pulled the door open. He held it open, keeping his eye on Merlin as the rest of the crowd started filing into the roadhouse.

Moving sideways for a few steps, Merlin then turned and headed for his pickup. He glanced back over his shoulder but no one was paying any attention to him now. As he reached the truck, the music became a muted pounding again as the roadhouse door was shut. Climbing inside the pickup, Merlin pulled the door closed hard, angry at himself that he's messed the whole thing up. He felt his hand shaking on the door handle and he looked down at both of them. He realized his hands were shaking from the adrenaline rush his body had gone through with the whole episode. It was exhilarating but energy draining at the same time. He hadn't felt that since his first army training and he wondered if other undercover agents felt the same thing when a fight broke out. His hand then went to his jaw and he worked it back and forth. The punch had been a solid one, especially since he hadn't seen it coming.

A moment later, he pushed it all from his mind. All the mattered was the fact he had to find some way to get inside and make contact with the militia group. The problem was he couldn't seem to stay inside, or anywhere outside for that matter, without getting into a fight. And so far, Brianna Long was the only tentative connection he had between the Chattahoochee Roadhouse and the Coal Mountain Militia. He shook his head. Even calling it a *tenta-*

tive connection was stretching it. The fact she was here at the road-house *and* she was from Coal Mountain may simply be a coincidence. His hand reached into his pocket for his keys as he tried to come up with another plan.

He had her Coal Mountain address from the Interpol report on the picture. Maybe if he started there, he could put together a list of friends she had in Coal Mountain, work it back to here and he could ferret out a lead–

A thought struck him and he looked over at the black pickup truck. Speaking of contacts...who was this guy she had just talked to? And kissed? If Brianna Long was with this Tyler Barnes–another thought struck him. The man had cocked his head and the kiss was more like a peck on the cheek. Or was it? From this distance, it had been hard to really be positive one way or another. Slipping out of the pickup, Merlin pocketed his keys as he headed across the parking lot. He glanced toward the roadhouse as he moved closer to the black pickup truck. He was curious about the envelope that had passed between them. As he reached the tailgate, he glanced back at the roadhouse and then put a hand on the truck, looking into the open bed. It was empty. He took a step back, looking for a place where the man could have stashed the envelope–

The door to the roadhouse opened and music blasted as several laughing people came out.

Merlin moved to his left and away from the pickup. He stepped between two other vehicles, trying to blend in with the shadows at the edge of the parking lot.

The group walked quickly to a Toyota, got in and were soon headed for the exit.

As the lights of the vehicle turned onto the road, Merlin headed back to the pickup truck. He had to find that envelope. But as he got closer, something else caught his attention. A round sticker on the back window. He moved to the side of the truck, looked around to make sure he wasn't being watched and then leaned to look closer at the sticker;

Tread On Me

An image of a coiled snake over crossed rifle

At Your Peril

Merlin pulled out his cell phone and looked around again before framing the round sticker in the phone's screen and tapping the icon. He wondered if he could get a good image under the low light but the phone's camera must have detected it was night because a flash lit up everything. Merlin cursed under his breath as he turned and headed back to his vehicle.

Laughter sounded.

There were a few people on the other side of the parking lot but they were walking the other way.

Reaching the pickup, Merlin climbed inside, pulled the door shut and then brought up the image he took to examine it. It wasn't anything he recognized. A quick Internet search turned up several other patches with a coiled snake image. A number of them had the words; Don't Tread On Me. Almost every patch was the insignia of a militia group, most of them anti-government.

Drumming his fingers on the steering wheel, Merlin pondered the possibility that he had a solid connection. Only one way to find out. He sent the image off to have Interpol check on it for him and then he looked through the contact list on the cell phone. But there was just one contact: Sunshine. He nearly laughed. If it was Director Aubrey Laurent, the man had a sense of humor. Especially considering his disposition. Merlin typed in a text message to 'Sunshine' and sent it over the I-24/7 secure network. He kept an eye on his screen for a few moments. There was no acknowledgment of receipt or a return message. He slipped the phone back in place and sat watching the roadhouse.

After a few moments, he pulled out his keys, leaned over and unlocked the glove box. Removing the gun from the holster, Merlin set it barrel down in a cup holder and then inserted the keys in the ignition without starting the engine. He was now ready for whatever happened, fight or flight. He sat back, letting out a small breath, trying to relax because it was probably going to be a long wait before his target came back out and went home.

After an hour, he began to wonder if this *was* a good plan. Then again, he had nothing else. His mind wandered a bit. He wanted to go and get a coffee but was afraid he would miss–

A knock sounded on his side window.

The sound startled Merlin.

His hand darted for the gun.

Chapter 11

AS MERLIN'S FINGER'S wrapped around the grip of his carbon fiber Beretta, he saw to see a black man in dark clothing and black ball cap standing beside the pickup.

The man stepped back a foot from the pickup, looked to the roadhouse and then rolled his hand, gesturing for Merlin to roll down his window.

Merlin kept his grip on the Beretta and his eyes on the man as he felt for the up and down control on the inside of the door. Finding it, he pressed down.

As the window slid down, the man glanced toward the entrance again and then his eyes locked with Merlin's. His voice was deep and gravelly, "Caleb Rucker?"

There was brief surprise at the use of the name and then Merlin gave him a slight nod, "Yeah."

"Sunshine sent me."

That surprised Merlin even more. He had needed fast action but hadn't expected it to be *that* fast.

The man moved closer. He held something in his hand and he held it out to Merlin.

It took a moment before Merlin reacted and took whatever it was from his hand. His brows knit together as he looked it. It was a black plastic box about one inch wide, two inches long and a half-inch thick.

The man must have sensed his confusion, "It's a GPS tracker that connects with your cell phone. Isn't that what you wanted?"

Merlin marveled at how fast it had worked. He had sent word to 'Sunshine' that he had needed one. He wasn't sure if the Director would contact a store and get one delivered or maybe have a trooper deliver one. And now he assumed the man was an undercover federal agent or an undercover state trooper...his wondering didn't matter. Because right now he had a more important question and he asked it, "Okay. How do I connect this thing to my cell phone?"

The man raised an eyebrow, "You're kidding, right?"

"Uh, no."

The man grumbled, "Who the hell sends someone out on an undercover job without – never mind. I'm not supposed to ask questions." He let out a breath of frustration, "Okay. The tracker is clean, no numbers or anything traceable so you don't have any worries if someone happens to find it. Now...did they give you a cell phone when they sent you out?"

"Yeah."

"Okay. I have an app on my phone that it works with. You should have one as well. You activate the app and just push that button on the side of the GPS tracker and it should connect."

"Should?"

"Hey, what can I tell you? I'm undercover, not a babysitter." He turned to walk way and then glanced back, "And what kind of code name is *Sunshine* anyway? Shouldn't it be Dragon Slayer or something like that?"

Merlin thought about his own last name and said, "I hope not. Anyway, thanks."

"No problem. Keep your head down." The man disappeared into the shadows.

Slipping his cell phone out, Merlin looked for some kind of app. There was a blue icon with two tiny footprints and he tapped it. Bingo. Merlin looked at the side of the GPS device, found the button and pressed it. The app on his phone showed it was rolling through some data and suddenly a map of the area appeared. A moment later, the screen zoomed in and right at his own location was a red dot. Now what? He checked the back of the GPS device and saw it had a magnet. Okay. That made sense.

Slipping out of his pickup, Merlin closed the door and headed across to the black pickup again, keeping one eye on the roadhouse door. Reaching his target, he scanned the parking lot and then knelt beside the back wheel. Holding the tracker in his fingers, he reached into the wheel well and pressed it up against the body. He felt satisfaction as the magnet locked itself against the metal.

Turning on his heels, Merlin rose to a crouch and kept low as he moved away from the pickup. After twenty feet, he straightened up, walked calmly back to his own vehicle and got in. Checking the cell phone, he saw a strong signal showing the tracker was still connected. He set it in the second cup holder, started the engine and left the parking lot. He drove slowly away from the roadhouse, glancing down at the cell phone. The signal stayed strong as the location began dropping behind him. He headed to the closest drive-through to get a coffee and wait for his target to come out and head for home.

Chapter 12

IT WAS NEARLY TWO in the morning before the red dot on the map began to move. Putting the pickup in gear, Merlin left the coffee shop behind, orienting himself and heading in the direction of the blinking red dot on the cell phone map. The roads were empty of traffic and it wasn't long before he estimated he was within a half-mile of the pickup truck.

In ten minutes he was on Highway 369 and passing a race track on the right. The houses he passed were dark and quiet. Before long he was passing over a long bridge and dark water below. There was a clack, clack, clack sound under his tires. When they were back over dry land on the other side, the sound disappeared and there were more trees than houses now.

The blinking dot remained at a steady 50 mph. The target was in no hurry to get where he was going but he was definitely headed in the direction of Coal Mountain and that was only a thirty to forty-five-minute drive from the roadhouse.

Fifteen minutes passed and then lights in Merlin's rearview mirror bounced up and down. A car far behind was going over a series of bumps in the road he had just passed. A moment later, a state trooper came up fast on his tail and stayed within a car length.

Merlin looked at his speed. He was just a click or two under the speed limit, so he was okay that way. He glanced several times in the rearview mirror, wondering if this was going to be the equivalent of getting in a fight at the roadhouse. Something always seemed to get in the way. Looking down at the red dot, he wondered how he would explain *that* if the trooper stopped him and noticed it. Being jailed as a stalker wouldn't please Laurent. Or should he always think of him as 'sunshine'? Merlin shook his head at his own thoughts. It didn't matter. All that did matter right now was–

The state trooper suddenly sped up and closed ground.

Merlin felt his gut tense.

Pulling out to pass, the state trooper's engine roared as he pressed the pedal to the metal and sped past. A moment later, he pulled back into the lane, his lights began flashing and he began to pull away.

His gut easing up, Merlin watched the state trooper disappear down the road, the flashing lights fading away. He imagined the trooper had probably just run his license plate number through his database, checking for a stolen vehicle or someone wanted on some warrant. He glanced into his side mirror, looking to see if any other vehicles or another trooper was trailing him – a thought struck him and Merlin chastised himself again. *He* should have gotten the license plate number of the black pickup and sent *that* to Interpol as well. Yeah, right. Do it all the hard way, Dragon.

Glancing down at the cell phone, he noted the red dot was still there. But it seemed to be more to his right than straight ahead. He glanced at the clock. It had been thirty-six minutes he presumed the man was getting near his home. He watched for a road to the right and sure enough a sign said the highway up ahead was intersecting with Highway 19. It was only another minute before he took the on-ramp and entered 19, heading northeast, increasing his speed.

Ten minutes later, the flashing dot was heading more to the west. An off-ramp came up and Merlin took it and then took the road heading in the direction of the flashing dot. The dark back-road was winding and rose to a higher elevation. Dark trees dotted both sides now and there were no houses or buildings that he could see. Merlin had to slow down. The unfamiliar, dark road made it harder to keep his eyes on the red dot and drive without going off into the trees. Five more minutes passed and he suddenly realized he had passed the red dot. Screeching to a stop, Merlin wondered how he had missed the pickup truck. He did a quick u-turn and headed back slowly, his eyes going from the red dot to the sides of the road. Finally, he came to a stop. The flashing red dot was off to the left. A gravel road led twenty feet off the back road to a large, horizontal rolling gate. As his eyes adjusted to the dark, Merlin could see a chain link fence running on either side of the gate through the trees, parallel to the road. It was topped with barbed wire.

Shutting off his lights, Merlin turned onto the gravel road and drove slowly to the gate. He got out, closed his door quickly to kill the interior light and checked the gate. The square box on the right side of the gate told him it was opened by a remote. Merlin peered through the gate and along the dark road on the other side. He couldn't see anything. Stepping back a few feet, Merlin pondered the thought of breaking in. He couldn't see any sensors but he had to assume they were there. Anyone spending money to put up a fence like this would most likely use intrusion sensors. He decided against it. For now.

Getting back inside the pickup, Merlin pulled back onto the road and headed back toward the highway. After a few minutes of thought, he pulled off the road and checked for Brianna Long's address. He entered it into the GPS and followed the voice as it directed him back to 19 and then toward 369 again. A few minutes later, he took another off-ramp to the right.

He passed a few large buildings on the left and right with large, empty parking lots. The map showed he was on the outskirts of the small community of Coal Mountain. It was only a few more minutes before he reached a T-intersection with another road and came to a stop. The voice said he had arrived at his destination. A large, century-old farmhouse was directly across from him. And parked in the long dirt driveway was the Explorer from the roadhouse. He was sure of it. A single light was on in the farmhouse on the second floor. Merlin could see a number of dark buildings further back on the property and he assumed they were outbuildings for the farm. Beyond that, nothing stood out as unusual or screamed 'militia'. The other property on the other hand did and he wondered what the connection was between these two people.

As he sat there, he also wondered; now what?

Chapter 13

MERLIN DRAGON WOKE UP as the sun peeked through the curtains. He had traveled back to Gainesville when he realized he couldn't find a motel in the small community of Coal Mountain. Everything was a half-hour away so coming back here and taking a room in a Motel 6 made the most sense. He showered and then realized he had now been wearing the same clothes for the last three days. Clothes that he had actually rolled around on the ground in during a couple of fights. How did undercover agents handle this kind of thing? He couldn't remember them carrying a suitcase in any movie he watched. He pushed it from his mind for now, turned his underwear inside out and got dressed.

Choosing the nearby Denny's Restaurant for breakfast, Merlin dug into a pile of waffles smothered in syrup. As he sat back, enjoying his coffee, his cell phone vibrated. Slipping it out, Merlin saw he had a report on the picture of the patch he had sent in. Actually, it wasn't a report. It was an image. It looked like a surveillance shot of several men dressed in military camouflage fatigues and camouflage face paint. One of the men stood sideways and something on the upper arm of his sleeve caught Merlin's attention. He zoomed closer on a familiar shoulder patch, but this one had a lower rocker arm with a name emblazoned on it.

Tread On Me

An image of a coiled snake over crossed rifle

At Your Peril

Coal Mountain Militia

He sat back and sipped on his coffee. He had an unknown man sporting a sticker on his truck that seemed to connect him with the militia group he was supposed to deal with. Seemed was the operative word since it was a loose connection; there was no name on the sticker.

Now what?

He had two addresses. One of them was a farm and the other appeared to be a gated compound of some kind. The latter was a more likely spot for weapons, which meant he had to find out what was in the compound. He doubted he could cut a hole in the fence or climb over without being detected but what choice did he have?

An idea came to him and he quickly paid for his breakfast and headed for his pickup. A quick Internet search on his cell phone led him to a large electronics store. He moved through the crowds, bypassing the game systems, cell phones, cameras of every sort and the newest and largest television sets that everyone else was concentrating on. At the far side of the store he found the section for the aerial drones. There were at least a dozen different models lined up along a counter. He looked at the nearest one called a QuadCopter Drone. The sales label said it had a controller and a camera. That should do it–

"Can I help you, sir?"

The voice was young and Merlin turned to see an eager-looking, young woman with long dreadlocks standing beside him. The name tag said; Brytney. "Uh, yeah. Are these things hard to fly?"

Brytney pursed her lips as she looked at the model, "Well, it can take a little practice. But they can be pretty sturdy, so if it crashes it shouldn't hurt it."

"Shouldn't?"

She shrugged, "It depends on where you crash it. A park is no problem, with the grass and everything. But we had a guy crash it on a highway he was flying over...."

"Right. Well, I'm looking at flying over trees and bushes out in the country. But I guess as long as I land it in a field, I should be okay."

"It isn't where you intend to land. It's where you crash by accident," she told him.

Merlin stood corrected and he smiled and nodded, "Right."

Brytney took several steps to her left and pointed at another model, "This one has state-of-the-art, obstacle-avoidance technology. The built-in sensors will keep it from crashing into trees and buildings and it can be programmed to return to the exact spot where it takes off from. The pocket controller lets you control it up to eight miles away and it has an ultra-high-definition camera. But—"

Merlin nodded, "I'll take it. It sounds like it's exactly what I need."

Brytney looked sheepish, "But what I was going to say was...the one you were looking at down there is $59. This one is $2099...."

"That's fine. Sunshine will be paying for it."

Chapter 14

MERLIN DROVE ALONG the back road to the rolling gate and then took it slow from there, following the fence line in the trees that paralleled the road and looking for a field or open spot he could work from. The problem was he couldn't find one. At one point, he couldn't see the fence through the dense trees and he wasn't even sure if he was still near the compound. After letting an SUV pass, he did a u-turn and headed back. When he spotted the fence line again, he made a decision and pulled over onto the gravel shoulder. This would have to do.

He rolled down all the windows and listened. Everything was quiet and serene. The heavy scent of the Georgia pine trees lining the road filled the cab of the pickup but there was no time to enjoy any of it. Making sure there was no traffic coming in either direction, Merlin grabbed the drone from the passenger seat, opened his door and quickly ran to the front of the pickup, the gravel crunching loudly underfoot. The small stones bit into his knees as he knelt and set the drone down. Removing the lens cap from the camera, he made sure it was on. Checking again to make sure the road still looked clear in either direction, he then sprinted back and jumped inside the pickup. Pulling the door shut, he picked up the controller and attached the battery. Brytney had shown him how to use the auto take-off feature and he turned it on.

A moment later, there was a loud buzz in front of the pickup truck and he looked up. The drone was already up and moving away, rising ten feet as it did. When it was thirty feet away, he took control – his heart skipped a beat as the little bugger took off faster than he expected. He tried to slow it by pulling back on the throttle on the controller – it veered to the right and headed for the trees!

Taking his eyes off the drone, he looked at the two joysticks on the controller.

What was it Brytney had told him?

The left stick controls pitch and yaw and the right stick controls throttle and roll.

Or was that the other way around?

He swore under his breath.

He placed his fingers on the right joystick and looked up in a panic.

The drone took off nearly straight up and barely missed the looming conifers.

It then veered right and began climbing over the trees.

Merlin's hand moved back and forth over the controls, struggling to bring the drone back over the road.

He lost sight of it and slid across to the passenger seat. There it was.

It took a long thirty seconds or so before he had rudimentary control and it leveled out. It was a just spec in the sky now but it began to grow larger as he brought it back toward the road. It took another long minute before he had it in a wobbly hover over the road. And then he cursed himself. He realized he had also forgotten to turn on the obstacle avoidance technology Brytney had told him about. He had been lucky.

Sliding carefully back across to the driver side, Merlin set to work before he screwed up totally. Bringing the drone up and over the top of the trees and the fence line to the left, he turned his attention to the video image. Which reminded him of something else he had forgotten. He pulled out his cell phone to make sure the app he had installed was still running. Fumbling with the controller *and* the cell phone at the same time was frustrating. But he finally was able to confirm he had the video feed hooked into his cell phone and would be able to record everything he saw.

Setting the cell phone down in the cup holder, he turned his full attention back to the drone. He slowly advanced the speed control and the drone began following the fence line. He spotted intrusion sensors along the fence as he had suspected, which meant breaking in would have been difficult, if not impossible, without being detected.

It wasn't long before the image showed he had reached the rolling gate and Merlin flew lower to examine it in the daylight for a moment. There definitely were intrusion sensors here as well. Carefully turning the drone, he brought it up as high as the tree tops and then began to follow the road into the compound. From what he could see, the property was heavily wooded with both deciduous and coniferous trees spread out below.

After three hundred yards, the drone broke out over open ground. The undulating road led another three hundred yards to a long, gravel parking area fronting a large, two-story building on the left. On the other side of the gravel lot were a series of 40 ft × 100 ft Quonset huts. A dozen dark pickup trucks and SUVs were parked in front of the first three huts.

Merlin flew high over top and then angled to the right to look at an area that looked familiar. As he drew closer he knew why. Far below was a rifle range, an explosives weapons range and an obstacle training and assault course. Over on the side was a shoot house, also know as a kill house. It was a structure used in training soldiers or swat team members in the art of infiltrating houses or apartment and the methods used to either clear the rooms or overwhelm the target in the quickest and most efficient manner. These guys were deadly serious in whatever they were up to.

Banking the drone back to the left, Merlin headed for an area where the ground looked chewed up. As he flew closer, he could see why. It was another training area, with foxholes and defensive trenches dug into the earth – Merlin swore. Several men in camouflage were on the edge of another heavily wooded area just ahead. And one of them was pointing up at the drone. Merlin flew the drone to the left and increased the speed to the max – he heard the burst of an automatic weapon in the distance and the camera image went black.

He waited. He listened. Leaning forward, he looked up through the windshield. Was it coming back or...?

Tossing the controller to the passenger seat, Merlin started the pickup, slammed it into gear and pressed down on the gas. The tires ripped up gravel and spit it out in a rooster tail before gaining traction and driving the truck onto the pavement. Now the tires smoked and squealed as Merlin kept the pedal down, leaving a long black streak on the pavement. A few minutes later, he realized he had made a mistake as the truck zipped past the gate and he saw it was rolling open. Merlin caught a brief glimpse of a black SUV barreling down the long road and he banged a fist on the steering wheel. He should have gone the other way. The pickup truck bounced hard up and down over the undulating back-road and there was a loud scraping sound as it bottomed out. Merlin could see sparks flash out on the road behind him but he kept the gas pedal to the floor. He had a small time advantage and he couldn't afford to give any of it away. He nearly spun out on a short curve. The back wheel hit the soft shoulder and the steering wheel was nearly torn from his hands. But he kept control and maintained his speed. He cut across the oncoming lane at the next corner. He did it again and then realized he could hit head-on with someone if he wasn't careful. He banged his fist on the steering wheel again. Being the 'good guy' could get him killed but he had no choice. He gripped the wheel harder on the next set of curves, fighting to maintain control as the truck tried to bring the back end around every time. He glanced in the rearview mirror.

The black SUV was in sight now. It looked to be gaining.

Merlin kept the gas down, fighting hard to stay ahead. The highway wasn't far now.

He glanced up again.

Closer.

Gritting his teeth, Merlin leaned forward, urging the pickup to go faster. Of course it didn't but he still tried.

The SUV grew larger.

Merlin had one chance. There was a hill just before the entrance to the highway. He had to gamble. But it would be dangerous. Not only to him but.... As he crested the hill, he took a final look back. There would be just enough time. He looked ahead. The way was clear. He waited until the last moment and then slammed the breaks on. He fought with the weight of the pickup again but managed to get it turned onto the ramp. But it was the *exit* ramp and he had to hope nothing was coming this way. His right wheel hit the gravel shoulder and threatened to send him crashing to the side. He gripped the steering wheel hard, offset the back end sway and managed to get the pickup straight again. Slamming the gas pedal down, he accelerated toward the highway. In a moment, he was driving the wrong way.

Horns sounded on the other side of the divided highway as drivers sent a warning.

But Merlin knew exactly what he was doing.

Or did he?

He glanced back.

There was no sign of the SUV.

Merlin felt some relief but he still had a problem.

Cars and trucks swerved to avoid him, horns sounding in protest at him.

He slowed and used the shoulder for a moment and then, when the way was clear, he did a hard u-turn and headed in the right direction.

As he approached the cut-off he had used, the dark vehicle entered the road on the other side. Its engine roared as it took off in pursuit of where they thought he was.

Merlin tried to relax but his body felt sore from the tension he had just put it through. He needed a nice hot shower. And a better plan.

Chapter 15

BACK AT DENNY'S the next morning, Merlin sat eating a breakfast of blueberry pancakes smothered in the house specialty, a blueberry-maple-bacon syrup. Skeptical at first, he had to admit the taste was as good as the aroma. But halfway through, his mind wandered to his problem and his appetite fell away. He set his fork down and picked up his coffee, setting his elbows on the table and sipping and thinking.

"Is everything all right, sir?"

Merlin looked up to see the petite, blonde waitress looking at him with concerned blue eyes and he sat back, "No—I mean, yes. Everything was great. I was just thinking, is all."

"Oh." She looked down at the plate, "Would y'all like me to take that away?"

"Uh...sure."

The young blonde nodded as she set the knife and fork on the plate and scooped it off the table. "Would you like some more coffee?"

"Uh...sure."

"I'll be right back."

"All right." Merlin sat back, contemplating his problem. Which was the lack of a viable plan to stop the Coal Mountain Militia from running guns up into.... Merlin ran a hand through his brown hair, realizing he had no idea on *where* they were running the guns. All he knew was they were supposed to be hitting gun shops in Atlanta to get firearms to sell on the black market. That's it. Lock, stock and barrel. Despite his assignment being a few days old, he had gathered little information. In the movies, it seemed they found out everything within the first day...no...make that the first hour. The hero met the girl...slept with the girl.... Merlin shook his head. He'd turned down the girl and got punched out twice. Some hero. The drone and the video popped into his mind and he pulled out the cell phone, wondering if he had gotten it recorded. Yes, there it was. He pressed play and watched it for a minute. Satisfied he had done something right, Merlin stopped it running, tapped out an explanation text message, attached the video and sent it off to Interpol to have it analyzed. Maybe there would be enough on the recording to have the authorities raid the compound and put a stop to what they were doing. Then he could go home. He wondered how Jigs was doing as he set the cell phone down on the table.

The young blonde server came back and refreshed his coffee. "Would you like something else, sir? Maybe toast and jam or marmalade to finish off?"

"No, thanks–" Merlin grabbed the cell phone.

Raising an eyebrow at his abruptness, the young woman turned and walked away to serve another table.

What Merlin had realized he had forgotten about was the GPS tracker. Was it still working? Or had they found that after shooting down the drone? No, there it was, flashing away and showing it was still active. The dot was in the northeast area of Gainesville. Dropping several bills on the table to pay the bill plus a tip, Merlin hustled out to the red pickup and headed across town.

He found himself in an older area of the city, tracking the flashing dot to a large block of rundown buildings. But it took him three slow drives around the long block before he finally spotted the black pickup. It was sitting halfway down a potted laneway on the left. Pulling into a parking spot on the street, Merlin tried to look as casual as possible as he walked back along the battered sidewalk, passing and ignoring the laneway on the other side of the street. At the corner, he crossed the street and came back, keeping an eye out for anyone watching him. There were a few people further down the street in front of a laundromat but no one paid any attention to him.

Reaching the laneway, he casually looked behind and then turned and headed for the pickup. The scent of urine and vomit hung in the air and then his senses were assaulted by the smell of rotting garbage outside what he assumed was a restaurant. He could hear the clicking of dishes and pots behind the closed door as he passed. The vehicle was tucked up against the back of an old, red brick building. The back entrance was boarded over which meant the driver could be anywhere. Merlin turned in a circle as he kept walking, wondering if he was being watched. He couldn't see anyone but that didn't mean they weren't there. Reaching the pickup, he took his eyes off the surrounding buildings and checked for the round Coal Mountain Militia sticker on the back window. There it was. He had the right vehicle. Memorizing the license plate this time, he hustled back to the street, checking both ways before emerging from the laneway and heading back to the corner, retracing his steps.

Back in the red pickup, Merlin sent the license plate number, the make and the model off to Interpol. He considered staying around and watching for the driver to come back and then following him again to see what else he could find out. But after a moment of mulling it over, he decided against it. He had no idea which building the driver was in and he could come back at any time. Or maybe he had a passenger. Maybe even one of the men he had gotten into a fight with. Either way, there was a good possibility the driver or a passenger could spot him and– Merlin shook his head at his own paranoia and the increasing scenarios coursing through his head. He started the pickup and put it into drive. This undercover work could drive you wacky.

IT TOOK THREE HOURS and seven coffees before a message came back from Interpol. Merlin called up an image of a Georgia driver's license. It was definitely the picture of the man he saw with Brianna Long. The name was Ethan Joshua Long. Age: 33. Height: 6-0. Weight: 202. Hair: Black. Eyes: Brown. Residence: Harrison Square. Gainesville, GA. He wondered if they were husband and wife. Make that *were* if they were living in two different places. Since there was no street number attached to the address, he called up a search for Harrison Square. It was a public housing complex consisting of 75 units. There was a report on Ethan Long as well and Merlin took a look at it. It showed he had attended Coal Mountain Elementary, Coal Mountain Middle School and Forsyth County High School. There was also the rest of the normal background information you would expect. Except for one big thing. The man had a rap sheet. There was only one conviction but it showed Long had served a five-year sentence in the Georgia State Prison. He had apparently been a model prisoner, excelling in an auto body and mechanics courses they offered and doing custom work for the prison. But Georgia State Prison was also the main maximum-security facility in the state of Georgia. Which meant a serious crime. Merlin scrolled down to see the sentence was for possessing a dangerous weapon; a recoilless rifle capable of firing explosive or non-explosive rockets. Merlin let out a low whistle. There was a reason the government was concerned with the Coal Mountain Militia if this was an indication of what they were into.

Merlin sat back and gave it some thought. He came up with a plan. But it was a 'way out there' type of plan. He just had no idea if anyone would go for it.

Chapter 16

THE NIGHT AIR was still warm as Ethan Long left the pool hall. The sounds of billiard balls colliding off one another and the drunken, slurred voices inside the pool hall were muted as the door closed behind him. He tossed his cigarette to the sidewalk and turned right as he headed for his truck parked down the street. He walked through several pools of light from a few weak overhead street lamps and then cut across the street to the sidewalk on the other side.

Ten feet ahead, a heavy-set, bearded black man in dark clothing stepped up onto the sidewalk from between two parked cars. The bearded man raised an old 45-caliber, semiautomatic pistol and aimed it straight at Long's head, His voice was gravely and angry, "I finally found you, you white piece of crap."

Holding his hands out, Long took a step back, "Whoa, hold on there, pal. I think you got me mixed up with someone else–"

The man took a step forward, jerking the gun at Long, "Don't you take another step! And I know *exactly* who you are."

Freezing in position and shaking his head, Long said, "No. You got me mixed up with–"

Cocking his head, the man said, "You don't even remember me, do you?"

"That's because we've never met—"

"No? Georgia State pen ring a bell? Does it? Huh?"

Long's eyebrows knit together strongly as he tried to place the man with the gun, "I'm sorry but—"

The man took a step, "You and your white power buddies screwed with me. You thought you could get away with framing me for that guy you shanked in the shower?"

Long shook his head in confusion.

"I ended up in Hi-Max because of you and your pals." The man shook his head, anguish and anger mixing across his face, "No one could come visit me. I didn't see my kids for years." He took a step and yelled, "My momma *died* when I was in Hi-Max."

Long took a tentative step backward, hands out.

"I couldn't even go to the funeral. Can you believe that? They wouldn't even let me go to my own momma's funeral. How could they do that to a man?"

Glancing to the left and right, Long realized there was no place to hide. The closest doors in the nearby rundown buildings were too far. And there was a long gap in the line of cars parked at the curb. He'd be gunned down before he made it to safety.

"I swore I'd hunt down every last one of you."

Long's voice was shaky as he spoke slowly, "Look. Pal. I'm telling you that you got the wrong guy—"

The black man straightened his arm out deliberately, his eyes glittering with anger, "Prepare to meet your maker—"

Crack! Crack! Crack!

Long froze in position.

The bearded black man's upper body jerked back hard with each shot and he grunted. Then he slowly fell over backward, landing with a stiff thud as the Ruger fell from his hand and clattered on the gritty sidewalk.

A moment later, Ethan Long turned his head slowly and looked over his shoulder.

Merlin Dragon stood ten feet behind him and to the side, handgun raised and pointing at the body on the sidewalk.

Long spun around–

Turning the handgun on Long, Merlin issued a warning, "Easy does it, friend." He glanced toward Long's hands.

Ethan Long held them up at chest height and shook his head, "No, no. I don't have a weapon."

Merlin nodded and then pulled his shirt tail out, wiping the weapon as he glanced around at the empty street.

"Thanks for what you did–"

"Uh, huh," Merlin said. He stepped to a curb drain at the edge of the sidewalk as he watched the street, "Just thought it was an unfair fight, is all."

Long cocked his head and narrowed his eyes, "You're that Rucker guy that hit on my sister."

Merlin shook his head as he dropped the magazine from the handgun, "I didn't really...never mind." He pocketed the magazine before bending over and slipping the gun through the oblong curb inlet.

Long turned in a half-circle, glancing at the body and then the street, "We should beat it. Someone will be calling the cops." When he turned back, Merlin was walking away, hands in his pockets. Long took off at a jog after him, "Wait up."

Merlin barely glanced at Long, "Why? I did my good deed for the day. Let's not make it more than that."

Long nodded as he reached Merlin's side, "Yeah, but you did me a favor. Now let me do you one." He glanced at the windows in the surrounding buildings, "Someone may have seen what you did and they could give the cops a description. Let me give you an alibi."

Merlin glanced at him as he kept walking, considering what he had said

Stepping off the sidewalk to the street, Long gestured with his head for Merlin to follow him, "C'mon. My friends will say you were with us all night."

Coming to a stop, Merlin glanced both ways and then looked at Long, "Your friends don't even know me."

"It has to start somewhere," was all that Long said as he started across the street.

A moment later, Merlin jogged to catch up to him.

Long glanced at Merlin's hands as they walked, "This isn't your first rodeo, is it?"

Merlin wasn't sure what he was talking about and didn't answer.

A couple of guys stepped out of the pool hall, pool cues in hand, obviously curious about the gunshots.

Stepping onto the sidewalk on the other side, Long gestured for the men to go back inside.

Merlin walked into the pool hall behind Long as he began talking to them about what happened and what he wanted them to do.

AS SOON AS THEY DISAPPEARED inside the pool hall, a man appeared on the stoop of a building just down from the body lying on the sidewalk. He jogged toward the body, the Gainesville

PD badge flapping from the chain around his neck. He knelt beside the body, laying a hand on the chest area–

The body grimaced and groaned. The eyes opened and undercover detective Xavier Grummett's hand flopped to his chest area as well. His fingers dug into the material and pulled a flattened, spent slug from the bulletproof vest under his now bullet-riddled shirt. He held it up to his eyes.

Undercover detective Kaleb Jones looked puzzled, "I thought it was only supposed to be *one* shot?"

Grummett nodded slightly, his voice hoarse, "Yeah, it was. I'm just glad that idiot is a good shot. But it still hurts like hell."

Grinning at his partner's discomfort, Jones said, "You didn't know he was a good shot when you volunteered, X."

"Don't remind me." He started to roll to get up

Jones pressed down on his chest, keeping him in place.

"Ow!" Grummett complained loudly, "Handle with care, Jonesy."

"Shut up, X. You're supposed to be dead, remember? The patrol cars and the ambulance will be here in a minute. They'll light up this place with all kinds of flashing lights and make a good show of it."

Grummett grimaced in pain again as he lay back slowly, "Yeah, yeah." He pulled at his beard and grumbled again, "This damn thing is itchy."

Jones pushed his hand away from the beard, "Leave it in place. Let's not screw this whole thing up."

"You're worse than my wife."

"You're divorced, remember?"

"Exactly. And just keep that in mind, *partner*."

Chapter 17

AFTER THE AMBULANCE left with the body and before the cops started canvassing the area, Ethan Long had one of his pool hall buddies retrieve his pickup and they met up on the next block, where Long and Merlin left the shooting scene behind.

Inside the Super Duty pickup for the first time, Merlin was surprised by the luxurious interior. The report said he didn't have a job so where did he get the money? He also wondered why the luxurious interior smelled of vanilla frosting until he saw a 'Cupcake Air Freshener' hanging from the rearview mirror. Strange thing for a tough dude to have. Probably a girlfriend's idea, which might me give someone else to check on if–

And then Long went and counteracted the smell when he lit up a strong smelling cigarette.

Which seemed strange to Merlin. Most people he knew with an expensive ride like this usually babied it inside and out. And that included not yellowing the interior with cigarette smoke–

Long realized Merlin was looking and him and he said, "Sorry, you want one?"

"No thanks."

"Oh. Thought you did."

"No, it's fine." Merlin was quiet for a moment as they passed three patrol cars heading the other way, lights flashing. He had to start a conversation and get things going but he didn't want to look to eager either. He shifted in his seat, "I have my truck back there. It's in front of the small coffee shop. I *was* going to get a coffee be-fore...anyway, if you take me back around the corner and the block over from it, I can–"

"Forget it. I can get one of my buddies to pick it up for you." Long held his hand out, "Just give me the keys–"

Merlin shook his head, "No. I appreciate your concern but I'll just get my truck myself and head on my way."

"No need to get touchy."

"I'm not...forget it. Just drop me off and I'll make my way back."

"Better you just give it a bit of time," Long suggested. "Those coppers are still working the scene and they'll be stopping everyone to ask questions. No need to test your alibi unless you really have to."

Merlin looked out the window, was silent for a moment and then said, "Yeah, I guess you're right."

Long puffed away on his cigarette, thinking for a moment be-fore glancing across at Merlin again, "Morgan told my sister you were a vet who just got out. You going to just keep roaming around? That your plan?"

Merlin shrugged, "What's it to you?"

Long's voice rose in anger, "Hey, all I'm trying to do is be friend-ly. You saved my life back there."

Watching the old buildings pass by for a moment, Merlin asked, "Who was that guy anyway? What did you do to him–?"

"Nothing. I don't even know who the damn guy was." Long forcefully blew out a stream of smoke that curled back in clouds off the windshield, "I was in the Georgia State pen for a stretch. Some-body must've screwed with the guy when he was in there and some-how he thought it was me. Or I was one of them."

"And it wasn't?"

"No, it wasn't," Long said forcefully. They road silently across the city for a while before Long spoke again, "Can I ask you a ques-tion?"

Merlin was quiet for a moment, wondering what was coming, "What about?"

"You serve in combat?

"Yeah. But I'm not talking about it." Merlin *had* served in a combat zone, mainly as support and training but he had been in-volved in several unavoidable firefights at an advanced base.

Long shook his head, "No, no. Don't get me wrong, I'm not asking to get any thrills. Look. A guy with your type of back-ground...like I said, this wasn't your first rodeo. You've been under fire. Hell, you blew that joker away and your hands weren't even trembling. I've seen guys in street fights or in brawls in the yard at Georgia State Prison who weren't as cool as you were after."

Merlin looked at his hands and then shrugged, "It doesn't mean anything." Actually, he was surprised at the observation, surprised at his own lack of an adrenalin rush. It was a fake shooting but he could have easily messed up. And even now, getting this close to his target should at least make him conscious of the danger.

"All I'm saying is the guys I run with could use a guy like you. Besides, I owe you. Maybe you just make a nice pile of money and move on, like you want."

Merlin looked across at Long, "You want me to shoot someone else?"

Long shook his head, "No, no. Nothing like that." Then he shrugged as well, "Well, if you had to. But no. Just sit tight. We'll be there in a minute."

"Where?"

There was no answer as they drove. Twenty minutes later they were in an old industrial area and Long turned left off a well-worn road onto a wide, gravel roadway. He drove in the dark for a minute before they passed beyond a gate-less and rusted chain link fence. Slowing down, the pickup bounced softly as Long drove across a pot-filled gravel lot. He pulled to a stop in front of a faded, brown brick warehouse that definitely had seen better days and turned the truck off. Long opened his door, "Wait here."

"Where are we?"

There was no answer as Long closed his door and strode to an old door. Light splashed out for a moment as he pulled it opened and then went inside.

Merlin sat in the dark, wondering where he was. Or more importantly, why was he here at all. He had left the special Beretta locked in the glove box of the red pickup after the undercover officers had given him a throwaway gun and he now felt very vulnerable. The cell phone was there as well so he couldn't even let someone know where he was.

The door cracked open, spilling light into the darkness. Long stuck his head out, waving for Merlin to come inside. Leaving the door open, Long then disappeared back inside.

Merlin had no choice and he stepped out of the Ford, closed the door and walked cautiously toward the still-open door, old gravel crunching under his feet. He went inside, pulling the door shut behind him and wondering what he was about to face.

The warehouse was a large open space, lit by a series of lights eighteen feet overhead. One hundred feet ahead, a dozen men were working around a number of large, wooden crates. Over the slight mustiness of the place, Merlin could smell WD-40 and gun conditioner.

Long was talking with two men. One was a large imposing figure, a couple of inches taller than the others and who seemed to have muscles on his muscles. The figure on the right was shorter but well-muscled as well. All three turned as they heard Merlin's boot steps approach

Merlin recognized the man on the right. He was the dark-haired man with the steel-gray eyes from the last fight in the parking lot at the Chattahoochee Roadhouse. Their eyes met and the steel-gray eyes went hard in recognition.

Long pointed at Merlin. "And *this* is Caleb Rucker. Caleb, this is Micah Blackledge. And that's his right-hand man, Gage Darosa."

Merlin and Darosa gave slight nods and then Merlin turned his attention to Blackledge, obviously the leader from what Long has said.

The big man stepped forward and held a hand out as he looked down into Merlin in the eyes, "Ethan told us what you did tonight. That took a lot of balls."

Merlin could see the man using his height to intimidate while looking for a tell that 'Caleb' wasn't who he said he was. He was also probing for a weakness. He hoped he didn't give either and Merlin simply shook the man's hand.

A hard grin crept across Blackledge's lips, "A man of few words. I like that." Then the smile faded, "Ethan said you're a vet and you could use a few bucks."

Merlin shrugged, "I got money."

"Okay, suit yourself. We just thought we could help." Black-ledge glanced at Long, who now looked a bit uncomfortable.

Gage Darosa spoke up, "You've got skills we could use, Rucker." His head turned slightly toward Blackledge and he said grudgingly, "This is the guy I mentioned, the one who took the gun from me."

Blackledge raised one eyebrow, "Really? That makes it more interesting. Gage here spent some time in the military and has some pretty good skills himself. You have to be top-notch to get the best of him."

Darosa's eyes had that hard look in them again as he listened to the words, perhaps from embarrassment.

Merlin shrugged, "I caught him off guard is all."

Nodding slowly, Blackledge said, "Maybe." The big man shifted on his feet, "Look. After shooting that guy, you might want a lot more money than you have so you can really stay under the radar. You did Ethan a solid, we can return the favor. Work with us for a bit. You might like what you see. If not, you move on."

Merlin looked at him for a moment before saying, "Okay. Just until the heat's off. And then...."

That seemed to please Long.

Just then one of the other men approached from behind Black-ledge, "Everything is packed away nice and tight, Blackie." He looked at Merlin suspiciously as he added, "We'll hit the road in an hour or so."

Blackledge nodded without turning, "Good. And Buck? Do me a favor and make sure you call G Money just before you meet up there"

Buck narrowed his eyes, not taking them off Merlin as he asked, "You expecting trouble up there?"

"Just make sure you call. You get any hint of smoky, you bail."

Nodding, Buck took a step back, "Got it." He eyed Merlin for another moment and then turned and headed back to the crates, "Okay, boys. Let's get 'em loaded."

Merlin had the impression these guys were still wary of him. And there was no doubt they were a hard lot who could turn on him in a heartbeat.

Chapter 18

SANDY SPRINGS, GEORGIA

MERLIN CAUGHT SIGHT of a sign, indicating they were in a northern suburb of Atlanta. There was a fair amount of traffic on the main highway for 3 AM but it wasn't long before they were driving into a quiet area of strip malls and stores.

He was riding in the lead van with Ethan Long, with three other vans following behind, two men per vehicle. Long had been quiet, smoking cigarette after cigarette. Merlin, a non-smoker, could taste the nicotine on his lips and his lungs felt a little heavy, resulting in him coughing every so often. If Long noticed it, he never said anything about it.

A burst of static filled the air and then a voice sounded, "*Long?*"

Long grabbed the walkie-talkie sitting in a cup holder, "Yeah?"

"*Crockett says he's ready.*"

"You got smoky on the run?"

"*Done.*"

"Okay. Get ready." Long pulled to the curb, set the walkie-talkie down and reached back between the seats, pulling a sack from the floor. He opened it and pulled out something black and passed it over to Merlin, "Put this on."

Merlin looked at it, realizing it was a ski mask. He looked over to see Long pull one over his own head and then reach back into the sack and pass something else over to Merlin.

Long realized Merlin still held the mask in his hands, "What's wrong? Not your style?"

Merlin paused for a moment and then pulled it over his head, "No. Just not sure what we're doing." He took the other item from Long's hand and realized it was a caver's headlamp, an elasticized strap that held a powerful lamp that allowed cave explorers to work hands-free.

"We're doing a smash and grab," answered Long. He slipped a headlamp over his own head, "This thing is set in close-range work mode, a wide beam with reduced glare so you can work in the dark. Don't turn it on till I tell you. Got it?"

"Yeah. Smash and grab what?"

"Whatever we find inside." Long handed him a set of gloves, threw the sack in the back again and then set the van in gear. He drove half a block before leading the other vans left into a large strip mall. Crossing the dark, empty parking lot at an angle, he led the way around to the dimly lit back of a long building.

Merlin was surprised to see a front end loader parked twenty feet away from the back end of a unit. Its lights were trained on the red brick wall and a man sat in the cab, watching them approach. The sign over the shipping doors said the unit housed The Old Georgia Gun Shop.

Long parked facing the building, about ten feet away from the wall and twenty feet to the left of the loader. The others vans took up spots to their left. Long opened his door and got out, "Let's go."

Merlin pulled the gloves on, jumped out, and stood looking at the loader, wondering what was happening.

"Caleb?"

There was a brief moment before Merlin realized Long was calling *him* from the side of the van. He had to be careful about answering faster to his undercover name or....

Long slid the side door of the van open and reached inside, pulling out a large duffel bag and holding it out to Merlin.

Merlin heard side doors sliding on the other vans as well as he stepped to Long and took the bag.

"There's a small rock hammer inside for you to use," Long told him, "One we're in, I'll tell you what to go for." Long reached in and pulled out another duffel bag.

Merlin saw the other men come around the back of the van and realized all six of them were also wearing ski masks, headlamps, gloves and each man carried a large duffel bag. These guys were well organized.

Long turned and lifted his hand, giving a whirling signal to the man in the loader.

The man gave a nod in return, looking eager to get started as he reached forward in the cab. The engine rumbled to life. Lowering the bucket to five feet off the ground, the man revved the engine and then slammed down on the accelerator, driving the loader forward and smashing into the wall. The bricks caved in with a hard thud.

Merlin glanced around at the dimly lit area. The back was lined with scrub trees that separated them from the back of another strip mall. "What about the cops?" he asked Long.

Long shook his head as he watched the loader back up for another run, "No worries. McLean used a burner phone to call in an active shooting by four men at an apartment building on the other side of this burg. By the time they get anybody routed back here, we'll be long gone."

That told Merlin these guys had not only done this before, they had it down to a practiced science. There was no telling how many weapons they had put into the hands of hardened criminals.

The loader's engine roared again as the driver took another run at the wall, this time smashing through the interior wall. Then he lowered the bucket and pulled broken bricks and shattered wooden studs away from the hole as he backed up.

Merlin glanced at Long, "You always use a loader to break in? It's kind of noisy, isn't it?" He glanced around.

A smile showed on Long's lips through the mouth hole in the mask, "No. We usually just steal a big truck. Something with heft. Turns out Tiny found this thing sitting at a construction site not far away and he just had to play with it. And like I say, by the time someone calls it in and the cops arrive, we'll be gone." Long reached up and turned his headlamp on before moving forward, "Alright. Lights on. Let's go."

The six men turned their headlamps and started after Long.

Merlin reached up, feeling for the switch and finally got it turned on. He headed after the others as Long led the way over the rubble and inside the breached building.

Long immediately began issuing instructions to the men. As they headed to their tasks, Long turned to Merlin, "You follow me."

Merlin heard glass breaking as he followed Long across the floor to a set of long, glass counters and display cases holding dozens of handguns.

Long gestured to them, "Use the hammer in your duffel bag to smash the glass. Pile the guns inside the bag as fast as you can. We only have a few minutes. Watch you don't get cut. All that does is leave DNA behind." He then pulled a set of bolt cutters from his duffel bag and stepped over to an area locked behind a wire cage.

Merlin saw Long cut the padlock off the gate and go inside. He then turned his attention to his own task. He pulled the hammer out and stood over the glass case, wondering if Director Laurent had expected him to actually participate in stealing guns. He brought the hammer down and shattered the glass top. Clearing the glass shards with the hammer, he began filling his duffel bag with weapons. It only took a half a minute and he moved to another case, smashing and grabbing. Glocks, Smith & Wesson, Browning, whatever make it was, he put it in the duffel bag. He was on his third smash and grab when Long stepped back out of the fenced-off area and yelled loudly, "Okay, time's up. Let's go."

Merlin threw his hammer in the duffel bag and zipped it. He was surprised at its weight as he struggled to carry it back to the hole in the wall. He noticed Long and the other six men were struggling with the weight as well.

Back outside, Long placed his duffel bag inside the van and waited for Merlin to do the same. Then he pulled the side door shut and headed to the other side, "Climb in."

Merlin pulled open the passenger door and climbed in, removing the headlamp and turning it off. As Long started the van, Merlin realized the man who had run the loader was gone and the loader stood empty. As they pulled away, Merlin looked in the side mirror to see one van following them and the other two heading the other way.

Long drove around to the front parking area and then took the road to the right, heading back the way they had come. After several blocks, Merlin saw the single van following them take a left turn at an intersection and disappear.

"You can take it off now."

Merlin looked at Long and realized he was talking about the ski mask. He had taken his off. Merlin slipped the masks off his head and brushed his hair with his fingers.

"How many guns you get?"

Thinking about it for a moment, Merlin shrugged, "I'm not even sure. Maybe thirty...forty. Maybe even fifty. I wasn't really counting."

Long grinned, "Yeah, I can imagine. It's your first time. A Glock G42 .380 ACP weighs just under a pound. A Smith&Wesson Sigma is a pound-and-a-half. The Beretta 96 is over two pounds. I saw a couple of revolvers in the cases you were working on before I went to do my own thing. You should have a Ruger GP100 double-action revolver in there that comes in at three pounds. Average two pounds per gun and if your bag weighs a hundred pounds...."

Merlin was surprised at the analysis, "You know your guns."

Long shrugged slightly, "Have to in this business. You can even make a quick bulk sale by estimating the number of guns in a bag and deciding what you want per gun. Six of us usually end up with one hundred to a hundred and fifty grand of guns in a haul like this."

Merlin didn't react for a minute and then he realized what he had said, "You mean $150,000 worth of guns?"

Laughing, Long said, "Yeah. But that's retail. We can get three to four times that when we take them up and sell them on the street in New York or New Jersey."

Merlin whistled.

"We can get up to $2,500 for an assault weapon. I don't think we got any tonight but we'll go after some on another trip." Long seemed to enjoy Merlin's reaction as he pulled out a pack of smokes and lit up.

Sitting back, Merlin's mind whirled. No wonder the man had a luxurious truck. These guys were rolling in dough. He shook his head as he looked out the window, not really seeing anything as they drove. Now what was he supposed to do? He was supposed to stop them from doing what he had just helped them to do; steal guns to sell on the black market and make a small fortune. Lives would now be lost because of him. Did he tell those undercover detectives about what happened so they could make an arrest? But that meant he'd have to testify and what proof did he have about what had happened tonight? Ethan had already supplied an alibi for the 'shooting' which meant they could all have someone–

"You okay?"

Long was looking at him, the cigarette burning away between his fingers, smoke curling to the roof.

"Uh, yeah. Just tired. It's what? Four? I haven't slept since–"

"You say you just got out and you're getting soft already." Long grinned at his own sense of humor and took a long drag on his cigarette as he accelerated onto the highway back to Gainesville.

Chapter 19

COAL MOUNTAIN

"**WHAT THE HELL** is *he* doing here? Brianna Long stood in the doorway of the farmhouse with her arms crossed and her legs wide, blocking anyone getting past her.

Ethan Long smiled and put a hand on her arm, "It's okay Bree. He worked with us last night and–"

"I don't give a lick. He was trying to sweet talk me while he was going with Morgan."

"I'm not going with anyone," Merlin complained. He was standing a few feet behind her brother. They were at the 'family farm' as Ethan had termed it, apparently in the family for generations and where his sister lived. He could smell freshly turned earth but it was mixed with the musty smell of old wood from the buildings out back that looked, in the light of day, like they might collapse at any moment.

"You know how aggressive, Morgan is," Ethan said to his sister, "she figures anybody she wants is–"

"Gavin is going to be here with Tyler any minute." Brianna jabbed a finger past her brother to Merlin, "And Gavin is on the hunt for *that* son of a biscuit on account he moved in on his woman."

Ethan shook his head and sounded angry, "Two peas in a pod, those two. Gavin's only taken her out a few time to—"

"That's not the point."

"Yes, it *is* the point. And I thought you and Tyler broke up—?"

"That's my business."

Ethan held his hands up in mock surrender, "Okay, fine. Just asking. Look. We just want to get some rest. We haven't even eaten breakfast and we just want to use the back rooms upstairs—"

"Take him to your own place," Brianna countered.

"You know I only have two small rooms and a small, single cot—you know what? Forget it." Ethan turned and walked toward his pickup sitting in the dirt driveway behind the Explorer, gesturing for Merlin to follow.

"Ethan," Brianna whined, "don't go away mad."

Looking over his shoulder as he walked, "I know the joke, Bree. Just go away."

"Ethan. Please." She strung the please out in a long whine.

Merlin took a step sideways while looking at Brianna, "Look. Don't get mad at your brother. He was just—"

Brianna looked hard at Merlin, her voice a low hiss, "This is *your* fault. If Gavin don't get you, I'll make sure someone else cancels your birth certificate." She lifted a finger of warning, "No one does this to my friends or my family. You hear?"

"Yeah." Merlin turned and headed for the truck. He wasn't sure if canceling his birth certificate was what he thought it was but it didn't sound good any way you looked at it. He pulled open the passenger door as Ethan started the engine. How many more people would he piss off before he finished this assignment?

"Don't let her bother you none," Ethan said as Merlin pulled his door shut. The truck jerked as he put it in reverse, "She's just been friends with Morgan since they was kids."

As the truck backed away from the farmhouse, Merlin watched her standing in the open doorway, arms still crossed, "She doesn't worry me. I'm just not sure about that Gavin character."

Ethan grinned as he backed the truck onto the road and then put it in drive, "Just blow him away like you did with that guy last night." The truck roared as he pressed down on the gas pedal and the truck took circled to the right and down the road, heading toward Highway 19.

Merlin pulled the magazine he had taken from the weapon before throwing it in the sewer, "Keep in mind I only have this left. What should I do? Take the bullets out and throw them at the guy?"

"It might work. Gavin's so dumb he just might forget to duck." Glancing at the magazine, Ethan asked, "Why did you keep that thing anyway?"

Merlin watched the trees and buildings whip by, "I put the cartridges in the magazine, didn't I?" He looked over at Ethan, who didn't seem to comprehend his reasoning. "Fingerprints?"

"Ah, right. You wiped the gun down but didn't have time for each cartridge." Ethan wagged a finger at him, "You're one smart dude. I would never have thought of that." He drove for a few more minutes and then said, "I'll have the boys put one of the guns from the haul last night aside for you."

Merlin nodded, "I appreciate that." If anything, that might give him something with a serial number and fingerprints that could tie these guys to the stolen weapons."How about if you take me back to where I left my pickup?"

"Yeah, we can do that. If we can't get some sleep right now, let's get some coffee and breakfast." Taking 19 to the south, it wasn't long before they were pulling in front of The Waffle House off Keith Bridge Road.

As Merlin headed for the front door, Ethan Long grabbed a newspaper from a vending box. He took a few quick steps to catch up and held out the newspaper, slapping it with the back of his hand, "Look at that, made the front page."

Merlin glanced at the front page of the Gainesville Times and the headline; Man Slain Dead In Street. He opened the door and stepped inside to the aroma of pancakes, waffles, syrup and hot coffee.

Ethan walked in behind him, reading through the article, "Says here the guy was identified as Kleavon Watkins. Served fifteen at Georgia State Prison and just got out."

Merlin glanced at Long as a server approached, "You know him?"

Shaking his head and obviously confused, Nathan said, "Nope. Doesn't ring any bells."

"Like you say, he must have had you confused with someone else."

"Yeah, I guess so."

"They have any leads?"

Ethan continued to scan through the article as they were led to a table near a window. He shook his head as he sat down, "Not really. Cops say they recovered a handgun at the scene that had the victim's fingerprints on it so they assume he was in a shootout." He let out a laugh, "The reporter says there are already rumors the guy was shot by someone he tried to rob at gunpoint. Or maybe a vigilante."

"Works for me." Merlin looked up at the waitress, "Coffee and a stack of pancakes for me. Ethan?"

Still preoccupied with the story, Long just nodded slightly.

"Make that two of everything. And he's footing the bill."

"I heard that, Rucker."

Ethan Long was still reading through the articles when the server returned with the coffee and plates of pancakes piled high, setting them in front of each man. Merlin slathered his stack with butter and syrup. Cutting out a triangular piece with his knife and fork, Merlin popped it into his mouth. It tasted great and reminded him of how hungry he actually was.

Long slapped the paper, "Not much else, but I tell you what...." He folded the paper, set it on the table and went to work adding butter and syrup to his own stack.

Merlin watched as Ethan picked up his knife and fork, getting ready to cut into his own stack, "Tell me what?"

"I'm going to reach out to my buddies still in Georgia State. If this guy just got out, they should know who he is." Ethan jabbed his fork at Merlin, "I also got a couple of guards I know who will do me a favor and look at this Watkins' files. I might find out who he *was* after and let that someone know. Could get me some brownie points I could use down the road. Besides, might be others of his friends out there who got me wrong. Can't be too safe. Right?"

At the news, Merlin felt his blood run cold and all he got out was a faint, "Right."

Ethan gave him a villainous grin, "But if my friends or the guards don't know, I got a secret weapon."

Merlin paused with his fork full of pancake halfway to his mouth, "A secret weapon? What does that mean?"

"I got someone on the string who can make contact with the very top. That's what it means." Long heartily tore into his breakfast.

Merlin set his fork down as he watched the man shovel food into his mouth with glee. Suddenly his own appetite was gone.

Chapter 20

MERLIN DRAGON WAS back in his own pickup, wondering how he could escalate this assignment. He had no idea how quickly Ethan Long could make contact with his prisoner friends in Georgia State Prison and ask about Kleavon Watkins. Or those guards he said would help. And then there was the 'secret weapon'. Merlin ran a hand through his hair. Long making contact with his sources was a definite worry. Because the truth was he had no idea if this Watkins even existed. He had left all that up to the undercover detectives and presumed they would have some kind of back story that would pass muster. But no one had expected anyone to even worry about that. And yet, this lack of foresight might just get him killed.

Merlin pulled a small piece of paper from his shirt pocket and slipped it into one of the cup holders. It held Long's cell phone number. Of course, he had asked Merlin for his, saying he would call him later to meet up again, but Merlin had no idea what his own cell phone number even was. He had used the back story of just getting out of the army and getting a new phone, but a small slip like that could be dangerous, maybe even get a man killed if he wasn't careful. Then again, what was the protocol for an Interpol agent - for a stopper - when asked for his number? Did he actually give out the number to his whiz-bang, do-it-all I-24/7 specialty phone? Merlin shook his head, laughing internally at himself. He felt like a babe in the woods surrounded by axe-wielding, mad-men lumberjacks who were ready to cut down every single tree in sight. And Merlin could barely whittle with a pocket knife.

Unlocking the glove box, he pulled out his Beretta from the conceal holster and that whiz-bang cell phone connected to Interpol's I-24/7 network. He slipped the nose of the gun into the second cup holder and then looked at the phone for a moment. He tapped it against his chin as he sat back. Several cars zipped by and the streets had more people than there had been last night. He glanced into the rear view, back to where the 'shooting' had taken place. A piece of yellow crime scene tape fluttered from a street lamp that had been used to cordon off the 'crime scene'. The setup had worked but it could all fall apart very soon.

The phone gave him an idea and he checked to see if the GPS tracker was still on Long's truck. The map popped up and the dot was still flashing on the screen. Setting it on the seat beside him, Merlin put the truck in gear and headed for the coordinates. It took twenty minutes before he turned off Old Athens Road onto Harrison Square. If he remembered correctly, this was the address where Long was living. He wondered why the man wasn't on the farm with his sister but figured it didn't matter in the long run. Harrison Square turned out to be a road that looped back onto Old Athens and encircled smaller inner roads and eighteen or so townhouses. Each townhouse appeared to be chopped up into six homes with just enough of a driveway to park a single vehicle out front. Merlin stopped and zoomed in on the map on the screen. The red dot flashed outside one of the housing units in the middle of the cluster. He took a slow run along the narrow inner roads, passing

Long's truck after a few minutes. It was parked in front of one of the units on his right.

Merlin had a plan. Retrieve the GPS unit and set it on a vehicle being used to run the guns north. Stopping the Coal Mountain Militia also meant finding out who was buying the guns and slapping them in jail along with the thieves. Shutting both ends made sense. Only a couple of problems. He had no idea how they were running the guns north, so he had no way of knowing if the GPS tracker idea would work. He knew they were 'loading' the guns at that old warehouse but then what? It was presumed they were using the Iron Pipeline. But what if they took them to an airport and flew them north? So he either had to get the tracker attached to an unknown vehicle or inside a case of the guns. Neither idea was very promising.

But getting the tracker back was first. The streets were quiet but it was broad daylight and he couldn't just stop behind the truck and retrieve it. He made a loop back around and realized there were two parking areas in the complex set aside for visitors. Each had eighteen parking spots. He pulled into the empty one and parked. Getting out, he took a quick look around. The day was warm but everything was quiet. He could hear children laughing in the distance. He vaguely remembered passing a small playground on Old Athens just as he had turned into the complex but he had been concentrating so much on finding the tracker that he hadn't really noticed the kids. He was going to have to be more observant. Another lesson learned. A small one in this case. But small mistakes kill you just as dead as big ones. Setting off at a casual pace, Merlin strolled toward Long's apartment. If he did this right, he would just look like a visitor and be invisible. And hopefully, Long would be as tired as he felt after a long night and be asleep already.

A moment after stepping onto the sidewalk heading for Long's unit, he divided his attention between the man's front door and front window, and the surrounding houses, watching for movement or evidence he was being watched. So far so good. Everything was quiet except for traffic in the distance. As he approached the back of the truck, Merlin took one last toward Long's front window and readied himself. As soon as he was near the tailgate of the pickup he pretended to drop something and squatted down to retrieve it. With another quick glance around, he moved low to the back wheel well and felt underneath for the tracker– the sound of a door opening and the strains of country rock music told him someone was coming out of the house. Merlin's fingers touched on the tracker and he moved fast. Pulling it away from the metal, he moved low to the rear of the truck and around to the other side just in time.

Sounds of footsteps echoed softly off the short sidewalk from the house and then they rustled over the dry grass of the small patch of lawn.

The driver side door opened.

Merlin crouched, holding the tracker in his left hand while swinging the right around to the back of his pants, reaching for his weapon– he swore under his breath. The Beretta was *still* in the cup holder. He was fortunate the huge, 8,500lb truck offered cover, but if whoever was on the other side of the truck came around to this side...or got in and pulled out of the driveway...either way, he was exposed. And his crouching here hiding and defenseless would probably get him shot. Now what?

Chapter 21

MERLIN'S BREATH WAS raspy and shallow as he tried his best to stay quiet, waiting for what came next. If the person came around the front of the truck and from the right, he could go left and behind the tailgate again. If the person–

"Ethan? I got him on the phone."

The woman's voice sounded familiar to Merlin. It sounded like she was standing at the doorway of Long's place.

"Where you going?" she asked. "I thought you wanted to talk to–"

Up inside the truck, Long grumbled, "Yeah, yeah, yeah. Keep your panties on."

"They are on. And they're staying on," the woman commented. "Now get your ass back in here."

The driver side door of the truck slammed shut.

Merlin could hear Long grumbling under his breath. It sounded like he was headed back toward his place.

"Whatcha doing?"

Merlin's head snapped around.

A little girl, dressed in a white tee-shirt and wildly colored leggings, stood on the sidewalk. Her eyes were curious as she watched him.

Merlin had to do some quick thinking before the one-sided conversation attracted the attention of Long or the woman. He still held the tracker in his left hand and he gave the little girl a smile and held it up. "I just dropped it," he said in a low voice. He rose slowly, staying bent over as he put his right hand on his lower back and took a couple of steps, glancing to his right to see if he was spotted. He caught a glimpse of Long at the still open door and the woman. She looked familiar but he couldn't place her.

"You must be old," the little girl said. "You don't look old. But you must be old cause that's what my grandma does when she gets up."

Merlin heard the door close and he straightened up as he stepped onto the sidewalk, "Yeah, there are days when I feel really old." He gave her a smile, "Gotta go. See you later."

"Why? Do I know you?"

Giving her a wave goodbye over his shoulder, Merlin kept moving. He slipped the GPS tracker into his pocket as he headed for his parked truck.

"Where we going?"

She was walking in the street beside him, looking up at him with innocent brown eyes.

"*We* aren't going anywhere. You have to go back to...wherever you came from."

"Why?"

Merlin shook his head softly, "Didn't anyone tell you you're not supposed to talk to strangers?"

"Yeah."

"Then why are you?"

The little girl shrugged.

Merlin glanced back over his shoulder. He didn't see anyone watching him from Long's place. And he didn't see anyone else watching him from a window or in the street. Yet, if this little girl ever went missing, he'd probably be the main suspect. How in the world did things keep going sideways for him? He stopped and pointed back down the street, "You have to go home. All right?"

The little girl stopped and looked at him, "I can't."

Merlin put his hands on his hips, "Why not?"

The little girl shrugged again, "Cause I don't live here."

Feeling frustration rising, Merlin said, "Well, go back to where you were and stay there."

Lifting her arm and pointing back down the street, the little girl said, "I was in the house where you were. But I can't go back in the house 'cause they're talking on the phone and it's private and stuff."

Merlin's blood ran cold. She must've come out of the house when the woman opened the door and was calling out to Long. He cursed softly.

"You're not supposed to say bad words."

"I know." He looked at her for a moment, thinking. "Are you Ethan's little girl?"

She looked confused and shook her head, "No." She pointed back to the house, "My mommy comes and visits him sometimes. But I have to go play, even when they just talk." Her shoulders hunched up and she looked put out, "But I don't have any friends here so I can't go play."

"Sorry to hear that." Merlin felt his jaw tightened. This wasn't good. If the little girl said anything, there would be a lot of questions and his cover would be blown. He glanced back at the house for a moment then and looked at the little girl, "Listen. I came over to...to look at Ethan's truck. I'm his friend and I'm going to get him a surprise gift. Can you keep it a secret?"

The little girl grinned, "I like secrets."

"Good. I like secrets, too. And don't tell your mommy either, okay?"

The grin disappeared to be replaced by big eyes of wonder, "Why? Are you buying her a gift, too?"

"No, I just don't want her to tell Ethan."

She looked disappointed, "Oh. Okay."

Merlin scratched the stubble on his chin, considering the situation. Then he reached into his pocket and pulled out a $20 bill, folding it as he glanced around again. Then he discreetly held his hand out, "I'll make you a deal. You keep the secret and you can buy yourself a present. How's that?"

The little girl reached out and took the bill, her eyes even larger than before, "Okay. Deal."

"Just make sure your mom doesn't see you with that *or* buying your present. Okay?"

Shaking her head, the little girl said, "No, I won't," and she slipped the money into the back pocket of her colorful leggings. She pressed her lips tightly together and made a motion zipping them shut.

"Good. Now go back and wait for your mom."

"My name is Madison. What's yours?"

"Uh...Carl. Nice to meet you, Madison. Now go."

"How come you can't remember your name?"

"Because your loud pants are blinding me. That's why?"

Madison giggled as she held one leg out, looking at it, "I know. They're way live." She suddenly turned and headed away at a fast clip down the street. She glanced back over her shoulder and yelled, "Bye."

Merlin puffed his cheeks out and let go with a sharp breath. So much for stealth in the Stopper profession. He turned and hustled away from the whole scene and back to his truck. Once inside, he set the tracker on the seat and sat back in relief. Now all he needed to do was find a vehicle carrying the guns north or inside a case or...whatever...he'd have a two-way case– it came to him in a flash. The woman at Long's door was the same raven-haired young woman he saw with Morgan Walker at the Federal Courthouse the day he took Walker's prints from the door push-plate. Who was she? And what was her connection to Long? What was the comment she made at the door? *Ethan? I got him on the phone.* If she worked at the courthouse, was she the 'someone on the string who can make contact with the very top'? The conduit for Ethan finding out about the shooting victim named in the paper?

Shifting in the seat, Merlin looked around and confirmed there wasn't another vehicle in the small parking lot. He put the truck in gear and looped around the lot and back onto the street, heading for the other side of Harrison Square. More than likely she had parked in the other visitor's parking area for the small community.

He found three vehicles sitting in the other parking space. Glancing in the direction of Long's apartment he entered the lot and pulled to a stop behind the three vehicles. Grabbing the cell phone, he took a picture of each license plate–

A child's laughter rang out.

It was Madison. She was running across a stretch of grass, heading right for the parking lot. And *his* truck. Merlin swore. She had spotted him and–

No. The woman from Long's place was running not far behind Madison. Her arms were stretched out like she was trying to catch the little girl on the run and she was laughing. They were playing.

Merlin put the truck in reverse and backed away, rolling quickly onto the roadway.

Madison headed straight to the blue, late-model Chevrolet Cavalier Sedan that was sitting in the parking lot. The woman caught her and there was a fit of giggles from both of them. Then the woman unlocked the car and they climbed inside.

Heading for the main road, Merlin used his thumb to call up the image of her license plate. At the stop sign he sent a message over the I-24/7. Glancing in the rearview mirror, he saw the Sedan pulling to a stop behind him. Putting a hand up near his face so the little girl wouldn't spot him, he glanced both ways, took a right and sped away.

Chapter 22

IT WAS LATE in the day and Merlin was in the industrial area, down the street from the brown brick warehouse where Long had taken him after the shooting. His cell phone was sitting in one of the cup holders and it buzzed. He grabbed it and saw information on the picture of the license plate from the Chevrolet Cavalier had finally come back. The car was registered to Rylee Johanna McDonald. Attached to the report was a driver's license complete with photo. He had only caught a glimpse of her at the courthouse, at Long's door, and when she ran for the car with the little girl, but the photo looked like the woman. Home address was Regent Landing Apartments, 200 Regent Court, Apt. 2, Gainesville, GA. Merlin closed his eyes. It sounded familiar. Oh, right. Morgan Walker was living in Apt. 1 at the same address. Interesting.

The rest of the information said she was working as a law clerk for Judge Otis G. McDaniel at the local Federal courthouse. Which explained why she was there that day with Walker. And more importantly, it lent credence to the possibility that she could reach out and help Ethan Long with his questions on the man who had tried to kill him.

Now what? That was the most pressing question. By now there was a possibility that Long had discovered Kleavon Watkins wasn't real. Or was he? Reaching out to those undercover detectives who had helped him made sense. Or did it? There was also the possibility he would blow *their* undercover identities and screwed up other cases they were working on.

Merlin set the phone back in the cup holder and took another look at the dark warehouse beyond the rusted chain link fence. There were no lights inside or outside. But then he hadn't seen any the night Ethan Long brought him here either. He was sure they would be inside though, working on the stolen guns and getting ready– headlights lit up the lot at the far end of the warehouse. A vehicle was coming from the back of the building. A moment later, a large panel truck rumbled around the corner and drove across the wide, gravel lot. As it passed through the opening in the chain-link fence and onto the roadway, Merlin recognized the driver as one of the men he saw inside the warehouse that night. The same with the man in the passenger seat. Was it a possibility they were making a run north with the load of guns he had helped steal? It made sense.

Waiting for them to get a half block head start, Merlin kept his lights off, pulled out and followed slowly, taking one last glance at the warehouse to make sure no one was watching or following. As the panel truck made a left at the first stop sign, he turned his lights on and made a rolling stop so he wouldn't lose them. And yet he did once they left Gainesville and hit Interstate 85, heading north toward Greenville, South Carolina. A Greyhound cut him off, obscuring his view. Vehicles came up on the left and kept pace, effectively boxing him in. Merlin chastised himself again. He had the tracker and a plan to put the tracker on the vehicle they would use to run the guns up the Iron Pipeline and he had screwed it up. He should have been around the back and found some way to put the tracker on the panel truck before they had ever left. He fidgeted in his seat and it took nearly ten agonizing minutes before he had an opening. He hit the gas, ignoring the horns blaring as he cut off another vehicle coming up fast in the left lane. The square shape of the panel truck wasn't anywhere to be seen in the vehicles up ahead. Slamming the gas pedal to the floor, he desperately searched the semi-darkness of the road ahead. A minute passed. Then another.

A bulky shape appeared down the road. A tiny flashing light lit up the back right side. If it *was* the panel truck, it was turning off. Why? They weren't anywhere near any kind of town. He had assumed they would stay on the highway going north to deliver the guns into the New York area. He kept his speed up. The problem was his truck wasn't the fasted beast on the road and he wasn't gaining. Once they turned off he could really lose them–

The blinking light winked out and the shape was gone.

Merlin pounded a fist on the steering wheel. This was ridiculous. The next time he went undercover he was driving a Porsche or a Lamborghini or something. He slowed at the last minute and took the off-ramp. As he wheeled around toward the stop sign for the crossroad he spotted the panel truck off to the left. It was headed north. Feeling some relief, he let it get a hundred yard head start before he turned to follow.

It didn't take more than a couple of minutes for the turn signal on the panel truck to blink for a right turn.

Merlin cut his lights and slowed to allow for the panel truck to approach a fifteen-foot high wire fence that looked to be more rust than metal.

The lights on the panel truck illuminated an open gate. Passing through, the headlights winked through the wire fence and then it disappeared.

Pulling to the shoulder, Merlin saw a dark sign just to the right of the open gate: Sugar Hill Metal Recycling. Why were they here? *Did* the panel truck have the weapons? He wasn't sure how stupid he should feel.

And there was only one way to answer that question.

Pulling forward along the shoulder, Merlin took a glance through the open gate. He could see piles of junk and a light glowing between the piles toward the back of the junkyard. One hundred yards further down the road, Merlin stopped, grabbed his Beretta and climbed out. The gravel crunched under his feet as he walked back toward the junkyard, slipping the gun into the conceal holster. He heard the truck beep twice as he pressed his fob to lock it and he hoped no one else would hear it from inside the junkyard. Running down the slight incline, across the shallow gutter and up the dry grass on the other side, Merlin jogged in the dark as he kept one eye on the road and one toward the rusty fence. He was puffing slightly as he reached it and began to climb. The fence sang a muted, rusty tone under his hands and feet. As he reached the top, he paused, looking for signs of anyone. Especially a junkyard dog. He could see a light burning about two hundred yards away between the high piles of junk and he could see movement. Dark shadows really. He quickly climbed down the other side and crept over to the first high pile of junk. From there he began threading his way toward the activity. The smell of motor oil, grease and lubricant battled the smell of rusted car parts and other musty debris he couldn't recognize.

Merlin reached a spot where he could see the panel truck. It was parked behind a large battered, blue semi truck and an open-top, metal-sided trailer. The two men he recognized from the warehouse were on each end of a heavy metal box and they set it beside the trailer. The engine from a large junkyard crane rumbled and the pincers at the end of the large arm were lowered toward the metal box. Once secured in the jaws of the pincers, the box was lifted and placed inside the trailer with a boom.

Two more men carried a second box from the panel truck and it was added to the trailer as well.

The sides of the trailer had round holes in the sides and Merlin could see five heavy boxes were already inside.

Once the sixth was added, the crane went to work adding scrap metal to the trailer. It was apparent the crane operator was being careful as he filled the trailer two-thirds of the way to the top. The last item that was added was a crushed, flattened car, topping it off like a strange metal frosting to a cake.

Merlin had a good guess at what they were doing. The stolen weapons were inside those heavy metal cases, taken from the warehouse to here by the panel truck. When the transport hauling the metal was inspected for any reason, it was highly unlikely anyone would be able to take out all the junk let alone the car and see what was at the bottom. Turning, Merlin headed back the way he had come in. He had to find some way to get the GSP tracker on that transport and find out where the other end of this particular run up Iron Pipeline was.

Chapter 23

THEY WERE BACK on I-85 North and Merlin followed the tractor-trailer at a distance, doing his best to stay awake and alert. He was running on a few hours sleep and a dozen cups of coffee. Which reminded him. He had to take a leak at some point. And preferably sooner than later. He had forgotten the age old practice of stakeouts and long-haul truck drivers. A bottle. He didn't even have an old coffee cup he could use. You're too neat, Merlin, just a little too neat. You had to dispose of–

The right signal light on the tractor trailer was blinking. They were turning off somewhere.

Wiping the sleep from his eyes, Merlin tried to remember if they had passed a sign for a turnoff or a truck stop.

The tractor trailer slowly moved right, the scrap metal singing a heavy-metal song in the distance as it bounced over a rough patch.

Merlin stepped on the gas and accelerated. He had no intention of losing them. Not at night.

The brake lights on the tractor trailer glowed an evil red for a few seconds and then disappeared into the dark tree line skirting the highway on the right.

His heart pounding, Merlin shifted forward in his seat, looking for any sign of the scrap trailer. As he slid into the exit lane he caught sight of lights through the tree line. He felt some relief a moment later when the flat, yellow roof over the pumps of a large gas station appeared. It was a highway truck stop. He slowed and turned right onto an expansive parking area, looking for the tractor trailer.

There it was, parked off to the right next to a dozen other rigs. The two men were already walking across the parking lot toward a large building complex that held a couple of fast food restaurants, a subway shop, a couple of coffee shops, a pizza place and some other places he couldn't make out. It didn't matter.

As he slowed to a crawl, he saw the two men walk into the first fast food place and head toward what looked like the restroom area. Time to act. He had no idea if they were going to be sitting down to eat or just relieving themselves, picking up food to go and hitting the road again. Merlin hit the gas and cursed himself when the tires screeched under the force. He glanced toward the two men as his truck shot across the pavement. They didn't react so he was okay. He turned his lights out and slowed, going around the back of the line of tractor trailers and parking in the darkness fifty yards away from the line. Grabbing the GPS tracker, Merlin slipped out of the truck and moved low across the pavement to the back of the first truck. From there he checked between the trucks as he made his way to the trailer hauling the scrap metal and the weapons. He chastised his thinking. He still only assumed the weapons were in the steel boxes under the ton of scrap. Slipping to the back set of tires, Merlin knelt and reached under the chassis with the hand holding the tracker.

"You want to check under my hood, sweetheart?"

Merlin felt his blood run cold. He also felt the magnet on the tracker grab onto the metal. Turning his head, he looked toward the voice.

A young woman, probably no more than seventeen or eighteen, stood at the back of the trailer. The moonlight glinted off the small patch of bare thigh between the tops of her stay-up, black stockings and the short black skirt. The blouse barely contained a healthy set of lungs.

"We could slip up into your sleeper cab and have a little fun. What do you say?"

Merlin realized she was a hooker. Truck drivers 'affectionately' called her kind 'lot lizards' because of their penchant for cruising from truck to truck at truck stops across the country, offering sex for money or drugs. He shook his head, "Sorry, but I have a problem here I have to take care of."

Lot Lizzie shrugged and gave him a bored grin, "So lie on your back like a mechanic and I'll fix your other problem. 40-60-80."

"40-60-80?"

Lizzie raised an eyebrow, "Now aren't you a bit of fresh meat?" One hip jutted out as she tried to take up a suggestive pose, "It's 40 for a blow job. 60 for a hump...any position. And 80 for both. It's just like the supermarket, sweetie. Take your pick."

"Uh...."

Voices sounded from somewhere in front of the tractor trailer.

Merlin cursed under his breath as he turned his head and listened. It sounded like a couple of men were headed this way. More than likely it was the two militia members driving the unit. He started back toward his truck but nearly bumped into Lizzie. He had forgotten she was still standing there.

Lizzie set her high-heeled shoes apart, trying to be suggestive as she looked into his eyes, "So you've made up your mind, then. What's it going to be, sweetie–?"

Merlin put a finger to his lips and put a hand on her arm, turning her gently and stepping softly across the back of the trailer. He had Lizzie stop a few feet from the far edge as he took a large step himself and peered around the corner. He cursed under his breath again. It was them. They carried a couple of fast food bags and each was sucking on the straw of a large drink. His mind whirled as he stepped back.

"Look, sweetie. If you're a little shy, you could close your eyes and–"

Merlin shook his head as he dug into his pocket and pulled out a wad of cash, "No. I just want to surprise my friends. They've been working long hours and...it doesn't matter." He peeled off $300 and handed it to Lizzie, "Why don't you head around to the cab and give them the works."

Lizzie looked at the cash in her hand with surprise, "Most guys can't do it more than once without being down for the night, sweetie. This is a lot more than...not that I'm complaining, mind you."

Merlin took her arm and moved her toward the edge of the trailer, "The extra is to keep my part a secret. At least for now. You tell them you're giving them freebies because they're so cute or something. And when they tell the story back at the bar, I'll bust their chops with the real story."

"Sweetie, you and your friends are a strange bunch. But I've done stranger, I guess. And it's your cash."

Merlin pulled back as he heard her high-heels click away on the pavement, heading for the front of the unit. Her voice called out in sing-song greeting and faded away behind him as he hustled for his pickup truck. If he had to turn over an expense sheet at the end, the one for 'Lizzie' would raise a few eyebrows. Then again, he could just call it 'party favors'.

Chapter 24

BACK IN HIS TRUCK, Merlin kept the lights off as he swung back around the rear of the transport trucks, noting the license of the scrap hauler, just in case, and then skirted away and around to the fast food place himself. He used the restroom and then picked up a couple of cheeseburgers, fries and a coke before heading back to his truck.

Setting his drink on the roof so he could open the truck door, Merlin glanced at the scrap hauler– it wasn't there. He whirled around, nearly losing his bag of food as he looked toward the exit. He actually couldn't see the exit because he was on the side of the stupid building and he cursed. He jumped in and started the truck, backing up– he heard the drink slide on the roof. He slammed the brakes on. A moment later, the drink tipped over, drenching the front windshield. The cup made a hollow bopping sound as it bounced three times off the hood and disappeared off the front.

Shaking his head, Merlin used the wipers to clear the mess as he backed up again, brought the truck around and zipped toward the gas station and the exit. He pulled to a stop on the far side. The exit was dark. There were three cars, a van and a dump truck at the gas pumps. But there was no sign of the scrap hauler. Then a thought struck him and Merlin slapped his own forehead. He had put the tracker on, hadn't he? Chastising himself for panicking, Merlin grabbed his cell phone and called up the tracker software. There it was, the red dot, blinking away. Zooming in, he could tell it was on the highway again, heading north. Forcing himself to relax, Merlin gassed up and bought two jerry cans for extra fuel. Then he went back and got another drink before setting out in pursuit of the scrap hauler. As he drove, nibbling on a cheeseburger, he wondered how Lizzie was making out. He shook his head at the unintended double entendre. And then he had to laugh at himself. He actually had no idea if Lizzie had even gotten into the truck with those two. Maybe she walked away with the easy cash instead. Or maybe she had made her pitch and charged them for whatever services she rendered as well.

Another thought struck Merlin. He had used the teenage girl without a second thought. Hooker or not, he had put her in the situation of selling her body and getting into a truck with two strangers. The words of Director Aubrey Laurent came back to him after he had been given a weapon despite the fact Interpol agents didn't carry guns; 'We chose you because you have a high moral compass, Mr. Dragon. Your psychological tests indicate you are a man who will do the right thing. Always. If that means using the weapon....'

Merlin wasn't so certain about his morals right now. He had always considered himself morally ethical, but the fact Laurent had been so confident he would use a weapon if necessary...or in this case a young hooker...made Merlin wonder if he knew himself at all.

BROOKLYN, NY

The trip up I-85 North took nearly fourteen hours plus these last two into a rough neighborhood in Brooklyn and Merlin was exhausted. It was still a couple of hours before sunup but the traffic was surprisingly heavy and he had to stay alert, not only to keep following the scrap hauler but to avoid an accident because he was tired.

After passing through a busy intersection, the scrap hauler turned right and before long they were in an old industrial area where the traffic thinned out. Merlin had to fall back to keep from being spotted and several times he pulled to the curb and shut his lights off, pretending to park. This last time proved interesting as the scrap hauler pulled to a stop in the street and one of the men jumped from the passenger side and disappeared off the road to the right.

Merlin could see the edge of a large wooden wall swing out toward the sidewalk.

A moment later, the scrap hauler started up again and turned slowly to the right.

Pulling out, Merlin kept his lights out as he approached slowly.

The scrap hauler was passing through the open gate of a battered and graffiti-filled, ten-foot high wooden fence. As the back end disappeared, the gate slowly closed behind it.

Merlin accelerated and then came to a sliding stop just next to the closed gate. The solid wall of wood kept him from seeing the interior but the faded sign told him what was inside; the Brooklyn Scrap Iron and Metal. Now what? A moment later, he put the truck in reverse, put his hand over the back seat and backed down the street where he cranked the wheel and pulled into an empty parking spot at the curb. Turning the truck off, he sat, looking at the wall of wood and thinking. Climbing inside would make sense. But it also didn't make sense. He knew where the drop-off spot was so there was no need to get caught trying to slip over the barrier and see what they were doing inside the compound. His assignment was to stop the Coal Mountain Militia from running guns up here. That was it. Where they went from here wasn't his worry right now. He grabbed his cell phone and checked to see if the tracker was showing inside despite all the piles of metal that should be on the other side. Yes, there it was, blinking away. He began thumbing a message into the phone. If the local police and the federal agents could get a warrant quickly enough and get inside, they could slap the cuffs on the ones receiving the stolen property, shut them down and keep the guns off the street–

The large wooden gate swung opened slowly and a man in a hoodie stepped out from the scrap yard and checked both ways before opening it all the way. Then he waved an arm in a circular motion to someone back inside.

The heavy, diesel sounds of a tractor trailer carried across the night air.

Merlin pressed send on the cell phone and sat up straighter, wondering if they were moving the scrap hauler somewhere else. No, the sound was deeper, heavier. Probably just another truck moving scrap out of the yard.

A black tractor trailer pulled slowly into the street, making a wide turn his way.

Leaning forward, Merlin was surprised by what it was hauling. It wasn't scrap– Merlin slouched down quickly when he realized the man who had driven the scrap hauler up here was driving this unit. Merlin put a hand up near his face to stay hidden from view, watching as the long trailer passed his truck. It carried ten or eleven cars. Merlin spotted a Porsche, a Mercedes– was that a Lamborghini? Yes. He counted three...four...it was past him and he couldn't make out any more. But a Lamborghini was going for $300,000 to $500,000. There had to be 3 or 4 million dollars worth of vehicles on the car hauler. What was going on–?

An orange, twenty-foot cargo truck similar to a u-haul pulled out from the junk yard and paused for a moment across the sidewalk, the driver watching the car carrier drive away.

Merlin was sure it was the second man who had brought the scrap hauler up north.

The cargo truck lurched and growled as the driver put it in gear and then it turned to drive in the opposite direction of the black tractor trailer.

The man in the hoodie stepped back around the gate and pulled it closed.

Merlin watched the orange cargo truck driving away. Then he sat up and looked in the rearview mirror as the car carrier continued moving in the other direction. The men had split up, each man taking another vehicle somewhere. Why? No doubt, there was more here than met the eye. The question was; what? And what did he do now?

Chapter 25

MERLIN PUT THE PICKUP in gear and pulled out, keeping the lights off. He knew what was on the car carrier. Presuming there was nothing hidden inside each car he had to assume they were running stolen cars from the people they sold the guns to. Not long ago, a luxury car-theft ring in the Bronx was caught and found to be a part of a sophisticated network of international thieves. In that case, the Bronx boys stole vehicles from the Kennedy and La Guardia airports, sold them to brokers who put them into sea containers and shipped them with bogus documents to accomplices in West African countries. In this case, the guys here in Brooklyn who received the guns were stealing luxury cars that the militia moved south, across jurisdictions and making it harder to track. It made sense. But the twenty-foot cargo truck was a complete mystery. He had no idea what they were doing with it. Or what was inside.

Following the cargo truck at a distance for two blocks, he put the lights on when it sped up and made a right. There was no way he could avoid being seen but at least he could trail it from a distance by following the tail lights.

The cargo truck maintained a steady speed through the streets of Brooklyn and then cut across the Verrazano-Narrows Bridge. The sun was up by the time it took I-95 south.

Merlin stayed as close as possible. He was tired but there was no doubt the driver was tired as well. Unfortunately, it took the other guy another three hours before he pulled into a truck stop. As the twenty-footer moved into the gas station, Merlin parked in front of a huge restaurant alongside a dozen other vehicles so he wouldn't stand out as he watched in his rear-view mirror.

His cell phone buzzed.

Grabbing it, he read the message while keeping an eye on the truck. It was from Interpol Washington, the national central bureau for the United States. It read: FBI and ATF informed. Agents now on stake outside of Brooklyn Scrap Iron and Metal and will track weapons and network.

Merlin quickly typed in a message regarding the car hauler that he assumed was headed back to Gainesville with a stack of stolen vehicles. He hit send at the same time that the truck pulled away from the gas station and headed back to the highway. He cursed under his breath as he backed out of the parking spot and followed. He had to take a leak again and couldn't because he had forgotten to keep one of the soft drink cups. Of course, how he would manage it while driving or in the open was another question. He needed a grizzled old partner to teach him things like in the movies.

The cargo truck continued south. The only deviation occurred just below Richmond, Virginia when it took an exit and headed into an industrial area.

Merlin pulled to a stop just down the street from an old warehouse just as an eighteen-foot by eighteen-foot door rolled upwards. The truck disappeared inside. He grabbed his cell phone and used Google maps to figure out where he was. This area was somewhere on the edge of Colonial Heights, VA. It didn't make any sense. What would they transport from Brooklyn to here? And why here?

Twenty-five minutes later, there was a slight rumble as the door opened again and the twenty-foot cargo truck came back out.

Merlin pulled out and followed at a distance as the truck retraced its route back to the highway and resumed its journey south.

It drove for another two hours before it pulled off into another truck stop. This time the twenty-foot cargo truck was parked in a spot designated for trucks at the edge of the parking area and the driver emerged, heading for one of the fast food joints.

Merlin watched as the man wiped at his eyes. He was no doubt feeling the same fatigue that Merlin was feeling. But this gave him his chance. Parking along the line of trucks, Merlin grabbed the holster holding the Beretta, slipped out, tucked the holster into the back of his pants under his shirt and headed for the back of the cargo truck. He took a quick glance toward the fast food place before moving quickly to the back doors of the truck– he cursed under his breath. The doors were padlocked. Now what? An idea came to him and he slipped his hand into his pocket and pulled out the bump key. He glanced around and then picked up the padlock and inserted the key. It only went in part way and nothing happened. Now what? Laurent had said you...what? Tapped the end? Yeah, that was it. Reaching around, Merlin pulled the Beretta and tapped the butt end against the end of the key. Nothing happened. He glanced around and then tapped harder. The key moved in further. The padlock was still locked in place. He tapped harder, twice. The key now turned and the padlock popped open. Well, what do you know? It actually worked. Slipping the padlock off and hooking on a pocket, Merlin swung the latch over, pulled the doors open and looked inside the cargo area. What the...?

Chapter 26

MERLIN DRAGON RECOGNIZED the six-foot long, brown-colored tube on the large three-foot tripod for what it was. He slipped the bump key into his pocket, stuck the gun in the holster and jumped up into the truck. As he stepped beside the tripod, he ran a hand over the tube. The number Mk-54 was evident on a metal label but it didn't strike a bell. But there was no doubt it was a recoilless rifle, a type of lightweight artillery that used a propellant gas at the back to fire a powerful projectile out the front. Most people knew of the 'bazooka', the common name for a man-portable recoilless anti-tank rocket-launcher, a weapon developed in 1942 by the U.S. Army that was held on the shoulder to fire. This recoilless rifle probably came from the same era but it was larger than a bazooka. It still looked portable but obviously needed the tripod to handle and fire. Which meant a larger projectile as well. But he had no idea what *kind* of projectile it fired. But the more important question was...where did it come from? And why did these guys have an old military weapon? The Coal Mountain Militia didn't strike him as collectors–

A noise sounded from the cab of the truck.

Merlin realized he'd been too absorbed with the old recoilless rifle. He grabbed the Beretta and tiptoed quickly to the rear of the truck where he listened carefully. He'd been fortunate. The doors had been left open but were straight out–

The engine started.

Cursing his stupidity, Merlin jumped to the pavement and turned, grabbing the left door. He swung it shut, being careful not to bang it. He grabbed the right door–

The truck ground into gear.

Closing the right door fast, it made a small bang and Merlin held his breath.

The truck began moving.

Merlin quickly grabbed the padlock he had hooked over his pocket and stumbled with the action. Crap. Now he had to jog to keep up as he swung the latch shut. Threading the padlock through the holes, he tried to lock it–

Speeding up, the cargo truck pulled away.

Stopping in his tracks, Merlin was sure the door was locked again. Or was it? Blowing out a hard breath at the near-miss, Merlin knew he had to hope for the best. Jogging back to his pickup, Merlin got in and grabbed his cell phone. Calling up the Google search function, he began looking for what he saw in the back of the cargo truck. It took him ten minutes before he found what it was...and his blood ran cold. The recoilless rifle he saw was a one-man portable weapon called the Mk-54 Davy Crockett Weapon System. It was actually from the 1950s and developed by the U.S. Army for use against Soviet and North Korean armor and troops in case war broke out in Europe or the Korean peninsula. But that wasn't the chilling part. The Davy Crockett Gun fired an *atomic* warhead with a 20-ton yield. It could easily take out several city blocks at the very least. But even worse, the shell's greatest effect would have been its extreme radiation hazard. It would produce an almost instantly lethal radiation dosage within five hundred feet of where it detonated and a fatal dose within a quarter mile. Even the person firing the weapon would be exposed to a lethal dose. The question again was where did they get it? No, the more important question was *why* did these guys have one? He didn't see any projectiles so what would they need it for?

Merlin quickly typed out a message, attached a picture of the Davy Crockett from the Internet and sent it off. Then he put the truck in gear and the tires squealed and smoked as he took off after the cargo truck. A woman standing next to a car at the gas station gave him a 'slow down' look but he ignored her. Cutting off a bus as he took the highway, Merlin ignored the blaring horns as he shot across the lanes and came back across in pursuit of the cargo truck. It took five minutes before he caught a glimpse of it up ahead–

The cell phone rang and rattled in the cup holder.

Merlin glanced at it as he brought his pickup into the right lane.

It rang and rattled again.

That had never happened before and Merlin wondered who was calling him. He hadn't given the number out. Or had he? No, he hadn't. With one eye on the cargo truck now only several car lengths ahead, Merlin grabbed the phone. It was a struggle to find the hands free button but he found it and pressed down with his thumb, "Hello?"

"Merlin Dragon?"

"Who is this? And how did–?"

"It's Laurent."

He hadn't expected that. "Yes, sir. Why–?"

"The Davy Crockett. Where is it now?"

Merlin could almost feel the tension in the Director's voice. "It's in the cargo truck ahead of me on the highway," he said. "We're headed south–"

"What about the projectiles? How many do they have?"

"I didn't see any type of projectiles in the back of the truck–"

"None at all?"

"No, sir."

There was a moment of silence and then Laurent said, "Mr. Dragon. The Davy Crockett was stolen from the U.S. Army Ordnance Museum in Fort Lee approximately two weeks ago–"

"That makes sense," Merlin muttered. He realized he was talking to himself as he watched the back of the truck and he spoke louder, "What I mean is, it was loaded on the truck in Colonial Heights, Virginia, which is just west of Fort Lee, sir."

There was a longer silence.

Merlin could hear the pavement buzzing under his wheels. He wondered if he was supposed to say something. Maybe offer to get the recoilless rifle back? Was that the protocol? Did he–?"

"The Davy Crockett used an M-388 round that utilized a version of the Mk-54 warhead, a very small sub-kiloton fission device."

"Yes, sir. I saw that in my research when I was trying to figure out what they had. The Mk-54 had a 20-ton yield–"

"They may have six of them."

"Pardon?"

"The warheads were supposed to have been disposed of. But a cold-war General decided he knew better and kept them under lock and key at Aberdeen Proving Ground in Aberdeen, Maryland. They were discovered when the U.S. Army Ordnance Museum was moved from there to Fort Lee. General Waters had passed away and he wasn't there to keep them as a personal secret. By the time the US government

found out about it, they were gone. All they had was the private diary kept by Waters to show where and why he had kept them."

"And that's why I'm really here? Why I'm on this assignment?"

"No. Not originally. We were genuinely interested in the Coal Mountain Militia because we had hints they were planning something big. But we had no idea they were involved in the theft of these atomic warheads. It's possible they're connected to another radical militia group the US government has been watching in Virginia but...the fact the Davy Crockett is heading to the group you're investigating...."

Merlin nodded to himself as he watched the back of the cargo truck, "It means their plans must include these nukes."

"It's also a possibility they're just a conduit to another group, like the one in Virginia. Maybe even terrorists willing to do what these militia groups would like to do. Strike at the government."

"Either way, it's a problem," Merlin said.

"Yes. And one you have to solve."

"Me? Isn't the US government going to move in on them?"

"No."

"No?"

"Isn't that what I said? We'll work on what we can behind the scenes. But the U.S. government can't officially be involved. Having one of their Generals pulling a stunt like Waters did would be a black eye on the administration. If the media got wind of a raid on the militia group, they would make it look like the powers-that-be don't have a clue as to what's going on under their noses."

"Looks like they don't."

"Welcome to the wonderful world of politics, Mr. Dragon. And welcome to the world of your new occupation."

Merlin heard the click and then the silence in the pickup was deafening. He was on his own.

Chapter 27

THE STOPPER WAS on his own. That was the reality of it. Merlin Dragon stood between...stood between what? A planned attack with atomic weapons on a high-value target by terrorists in a major city? Like what happened with the planes and the Twin Towers in New York? Or an imminent threat against a target where the recoilless rifle was headed? Was it someone the Coal Mountain Militia had a grudge against in the Gainesville area? That didn't make any sense. Then again, if these guys knew the person firing the weapon would probably die as well, common sense didn't have anything to do with it.

Merlin watched the back of the cargo truck, all the scenarios going through his mind. If he stopped the truck and beat the crap out of the guy, what happens if the driver had no idea where the warheads were? And then if the Davey Crockett isn't delivered, the militia knows something is wrong, move the warheads and maybe steal another Davey Crockett held in some other museum. Or maybe they modify another recoilless rifle to use. Or find another way. No, it would only slow them down in their plans, not stop them.

Then again, if he waited and lost track of the cargo truck, then what? It seemed no matter what he did, it could blow up on him.

What was it that Laurent had said that sounded so appealing to him at the start? *'From here on, you make all the decisions. Out there in the field, you decide on what to do...you work alone.'* Yeah, welcome to your new reality, Dragon.

Merlin made a decision to sit tight. If he could stick with the cargo truck right to its destination, he would have a few more answers and a few more people to work on. No, make that *should* because there were no guarantees in a situation like this.

The cargo truck stopped once more a couple of hours north of Gainesville. The driver parked in an area away from other vehicles but stayed in the truck this time.

Merlin was sure he saw the driver put his seat back and pull a ball cap low over his eyes. There was no doubt the driver was fatigued because Merlin certainly felt it. The problem was he couldn't grab some shut-eye and risk missing the truck getting back on the road. All he could do was pull up to a coffee shop where he could keep an eye on the cargo truck, grab a couple of large coffees, several sandwiches, and a dozen donuts and get back inside the pickup truck. And this time he would keep the cups to relieve himself.

Hours passed before the driver finally stirred and got out of the truck, heading for the 24-hour coffee shop.

When Merlin saw the man stand at the end of the long line of customers, he quickly slipped inside and used the washroom. Splashing cold water on his face before heading back out, Merlin felt like a new man. Well, maybe not new, just not so stale. The driver was just ordering his own coffee, sandwiches, and donuts for dessert when Merlin slipped back out to the pickup and waited.

Getting back in the cargo truck, the driver wolfed down his sandwiches, washing it down with coffee. Then munching on a donut, he made his way back to the highway and continued his journey in the small hours of the morning.

Merlin followed, keeping at least one car between him and the cargo truck. He fell back every so often, switching lanes and hiding behind a larger vehicle from time to time but he was afraid to be too cautious. He tried to keep the hide and seek between exits, but beyond that, he couldn't afford to make a mistake and lose his only link to the atomic weapons.

Chapter 28

BY THE TIME the cargo truck reached the Gainesville area again, Merlin was more than spent. He realized it had been well over...what? A day? A day and a half? He couldn't remember the last he had slept and the smell of the now-stale coffee and half-eaten, stale sandwich bothered him more than he thought it would. He kept wondering if he was cut out for this life and then just pushed that thought aside as part of the fog of fatigue–

In the rearview mirror he saw flashing lights come out of the dark distance and close fast.

It was the Georgia State Patrol.

Merlin's mind went through all his driving maneuvers...he hadn't changed lanes without signaling...he wasn't speeding...in fact, for the last half hour he had stayed two cars back of the cargo truck at five clicks under the limit.

The flashing lights didn't pull over to pass. They came up on his bumper and stayed there. *He* was their target.

He had no choice. Hopefully, this was just a routine stop and he could move on after the truck before long. Flipping on the turn signal, Merlin slowed the pickup and pulled to the paved shoulder. He cursed as he came to a stop, watching the rear lights of the cargo truck disappear down the highway. One of the things he couldn't afford was awkward questions and he had no way of proving who he was and he could lose valuable time. He discreetly moved his hand to the Beretta and slipped it under the seat. He did the same with the cell phone as he looked down into the side mirror.

The driver side door of the patrol car swing open and a husky state trooper stepped out and closed the door. He glanced back down the highway as several vehicles switched lanes to go past the flashing lights. Then the trooper looked back at the red pickup truck. A moment later, his attention went to the opposite lane of traffic.

Merlin heard another door shut and his own attention went to the rearview mirror. There was a second trooper on the passenger side. That struck Merlin as odd. Most troopers worked in a car alone.

The state trooper on the driver side moved to the rear of the pickup and spoke loudly, "Can you step out of the car, sir?"

Merlin saw the trooper glance ahead and then back down the highway again. Setting his hand on the door handle, Merlin's senses heightened and he felt something was off. But he couldn't put a finger on it. Opening the door, he checked for traffic and then got out, closing it gently. The night air was warm and carried the scent of the pine trees on the sides of the highway, mingling with the smell of diesel, gasoline, and motor oil from the highway. He couldn't help but glance at where the cargo truck had disappeared and he wondered if telling the troopers who he was would take long to get it checked out and–

"Put your attention this way, pal."

That was the second trooper who had taken up a position between the two vehicles. He gestured for Merlin to head his way.

Merlin complied, moving slowly toward the back of his truck.

When he got there, the trooper on the driver side stepped forward, took Merlin's elbow and turned him, "Face the back of the truck and put your hands behind your back."

He did as he was told and then Merlin was surprised as he felt the cold steel of handcuffs around his wrists and the sound of them being ratcheted tight. He looked over his shoulder, "Can I ask what this is about?"

"You'll know soon enough," the second trooper said.

The first trooper took Merlin's elbow again and turned him toward the patrol car, "This way."

As Merlin walked along the edge of the highway, he tried to figure out what was happening. Maybe someone saw him with the weapon and reported it. Again, he debated how much he should tell them–

The trunk on the patrol car popped up.

Merlin glanced into the patrol car and something else struck him as odd. But before he even had time to figure out what it was, he was surprised when the trooper kept him moving past the back door of the car to the rear of the vehicle and the open trunk. He had assumed he would be placed in the back seat. But he wasn't. He was turned to face the open trunk and then was patted down quickly by the second trooper who took his cash and license.

The first trooper kept watching both ways along the highway, keeping an eye on the traffic. A moment later, as the trooper behind Merlin stood up, the first trooper simply said, "Okay."

Pushed hard from behind, Merlin fell forward into the trunk, his forehead banging hard against the floor. His legs were shoved roughly over the edge of the trunk and the lid was slammed shut. Shaking his head, Merlin tried to clear the light fog from the blow to his head, wondering what was happening. None of this made any sense. He heard the troopers talking. No, it was just one talking.

"Yeah, he's in the trunk. No, we haven't checked the pickup yet. Yeah. His driver's license says he's Caleb Rucker. That's right, Caleb Rucker. The address is 36 Peachtree Road down in Atlanta–"

Merlin heard silence and then low cursing.

"No. He's just got a wad of cash on him. You want me to find out why he was followin' or...?"

Cursing himself now, Merlin realized he had been spotted following the cargo truck. Or maybe it was before. Some undercover agent he was–

"Okay. We'll take care of him first, come back for the truck later."

There was a moment of silence and then there was the sound of two car doors slamming shut and Merlin felt the vibration through the frame. A moment later, the car's engine started, revved and Merlin felt the car turn and move. The low growl of tires over pavement told him they were moving fast down the highway. He had a feeling he wasn't headed to a jail cell or an interrogation room. Now what?

Chapter 29

NOW ALL THAT training and preparation in the army and the small kit he was given on the plane made sense. *This* was why. As he lay on his side, he pulled his boots up toward his hands and felt with his fingers for the blacked-brass tip on the shoelaces. And more specifically, for the hand cuff key. He tugged on one end, loosening the lace and getting enough slack to insert the key and—

The patrol car hit a bump and the key dropped from his fingers. Panic set in.

Until he realized he hadn't pulled the key right off the lace and all the had to do feel for it again. And even if he had pulled it off, how far could it go inside a locked trunk? He laughed at himself as he found the key and inserted it...the key worked! The cuffs unlocked and he rolled over, removing them from his wrists. Pushing them to the side, he rubbed his wrists and tried to formulate a plan. The problem was he was limited in what he could do. He considered pulling up the flap in the trunk floor to access the spare tire area and the tire iron that would be under there. That could serve as a weapon. But as he moved around, he realized there just wasn't enough room to get the flap up enough. He was able to snake a hand underneath to the tire but there was no way he could get it out of the way to access the iron underneath. Setting the flap down, he next considered getting the trunk open. Then what? Jumping out on the highway at this speed would be suicide. Even if he survived the 'drop and roll' on the pavement, he would probably be run over by another vehicle. Or end up being stunned by the fall, the troopers see him rolling on the pavement and go back and get him. Nope. All he could do was wait. Besides, if he did get out of this, he needed to know how to get back to his truck. For now, he concentrated on the movements of the car and the passage of time.

After twenty minutes, the car slowed and there was no doubt they left the highway. And from the turns the vehicle made, they headed south. Approximately twenty-five minutes passed before Merlin felt the vehicle come to a stop, turn left and start traveling over a rougher road. Five minutes later, it slowed again and turned right. From the bumps, it certainly didn't feel like they had turned into any parking lot for a trooper station.

When he felt the vehicle come to a stop and the engine turned off, he grabbed the handcuffs and held them so that the metal was wrapped over the knuckles of his right hand. It was his only weapon– no, that was wrong. He slipped the cuffs over his left hand and dug into his back pocket for the American Liberty nickel.

A car door slammed shut.

Finding the coin, Merlin pulled it out

A second car door slammed.

Merlin felt with his fingers to find the head side, held the coin heads-up, slid his fingernail clockwise along the edge and the small blade of hardened stainless steel rotated out. He held that between the thumb and forefinger of his right hand as he slid around and crouched on his knees in the tight space.

Voices sounded outside the back of the vehicle.

The trunk popped up.

In the darkness, one of the troopers bent over to grab the prisoner and Merlin struck, driving his left hand and the make-shift 'brass-knuckles' into the man's throat.

The soft crunch of cartilage breaking sounded just before a gurgle from the troopers mouth. He grabbed his throat and staggered back, falling backward with a thud

The second trooper, holding a gun and standing just to the right of the trunk, was startled and took a half-step back. It took a second before he moved to bring the gun up.

That brief hesitation gave Merlin his chance and he launched himself forward, sweeping his right hand across the trooper's gun hand. The small blade sliced at an angle across the man's gun hand, biting deep.

The trooper howled and dropped his gun, clutching at his hand as the blood spurted.

Merlin used his momentum to flip over the lower edge of the trunk. But he made a mistake by letting his legs extend too much and his boots hit the trunk lid just enough to blunt his effort. He landed straight down on his head, grunting from the blow.

The trooper cursed hard at the prisoner and he bent over to retrieve his weapon as he still held onto the bloody hand.

It gave Merlin that extra split second he needed. He twisted around on the ground, the handcuffs jangling softly as he threw an uppercut.

Hit straight on the chin, the trooper dropped like a stone on top of his attacker

Merlin felt the air driven from his lungs and it stunned him for a moment. Then he worked to push the unconscious trooper off him, coughing from the effort as his bruised lungs protested. Getting to his knees, he grabbed the handgun from the ground where the second trooper had dropped it and stuck it in his belt. Returning the blade to its hiding place in the coin, he put the nickel in his back pocket again and then he crawled to the other trooper, removing the weapon from his holster. He double-checked the neck pulse. Dead. He wondered how he would explain one dead trooper and one unconscious one.

He would have to deal with that later. Grabbing a second set of cuffs from the dead trooper, Merlin used the two sets to secure the wrists and feet of the unconscious trooper. Then he manhandled the dead trooper into the trunk and then the second one on top of him. He leaned on the edge of the trunk, breathing heavy and thinking. Now how was he going to figure out where the cargo truck carrying the Davey Crockett went? And how could he find the atomic projectiles if he couldn't track the recoilless rifle to whoever was going to use it? This was a mess. Could the Stopper be fired? Oh, right. Laurent said they would just take him into the woods and shoot him. Simple enough.

And then, as he looked at the bodies of the two troopers, the sense of something being odd or off washed over him again. The question was; what was it?

Chapter 30

AND THEN IT hit Merlin. He moved quickly to the side of the vehicle and pulled the driver side door open. Just as he had thought. When the troopers had first moved him toward the back of the vehicle along the highway, he had glanced inside and something only half registered. But now he knew what it was. The interior was plain and simple. There was no sign of any police equipment. No computer, no siren controls or the protective plastic screen between the front and back seats you usually see. The keys were still in the ignition but he noticed something else. There was a toggle switch on the steering column and he flicked it up. The lights on the top of the vehicle began flashing and the headlights did a back and force dance of splashing light into the darkness ahead. He flicked the toggle switch to off, slammed the door shut and looked at the outside of it. Running his hand along the words 'Georgia State Patrol' and the logo over top, he could feel the edges of a sticker. Merlin cursed under his breath. These guys weren't real troopers. Or maybe they *were* real troopers but were using a dummy car to get rid of him. That would make sense. No forensics in their real patrol car to tie them to his body. *If* it was found. And there would be no GPS trail on a regular patrol car's navigation system that tied them back to this spot. But none of that helped him right now.

Or did it?

They didn't have a police radio to call out.

And yet they were talking to someone…he heard them *outside* the trunk when he was in there.

They were using a cell phone.

He had assumed they were talking to a dispatcher but that wasn't likely and he had nearly missed it.

Merlin rushed back to the still open trunk and began searching the unconscious trooper. Nothing. He struggled to search the one underneath. Bingo. He found an iPhone in one of his pockets. There were no phone numbers in the contact list but the last number dialed was on the screen. It was a long shot but he had some hope. He slammed the trunk shut and climbed into the car where he turned on the flashing overhead lights. The headlights began their back and forth dance as he began driving. He realized he was on a back road surrounded on both sides by dark trees. He wondered if his body would have ever been found and then he pushed that thought out of his mind. He had to concentrate on remembering the movements of the patrol car, tied to the passage of time, and finding his way back to the highway.

He made only one wrong turn, ending up on a dead end back road but he finally found the highway and sped back in the direction of his pickup. He passed it on the other side, took the next turnaround and came back to park behind it, turning off the vehicle and cutting the flashing lights and the headlights.

Hustling into the pickup, Merlin set the trooper's weapons on the passenger seat, pulled out the Beretta and his own cell phone and composed a message explaining the entire situation. That done, he sat there for a moment, considering what to do next. He glanced into the rearview mirror and decided getting away from the fake patrol car with the two troopers in the trunk was the first priority. Once the way was clear, Merlin pulled onto the highway and sped away as he wondered how many people might die because he had lost contact with the cargo truck and the Davy Crockett.

Chapter 31

THE SUN WAS UP and Merlin sat in the parking lot of a coffee shop on the edge of Gainesville, coffee cup in one hand and sugar donut in the other. It had been more than two hours since he had sent the message and he had already gone through the drive-through three times, hoping the surge of caffeine and the hits of sugar would keep him awake. It had long gone past the point of fighting with the fatigue. He was trying to be a friend of it, trying to fool it. He breathed in the deep rich scent of the coffee, half kidding himself that the caffeine molecules in the air might even be stronger–

The cell phone buzzed and danced lightly in the cup holder.

Grabbing it quickly, Merlin found a text message: FBI on scene of fake state patrol car; confirmed and will deal with the situation. Number is from a disposable cell phone, no contract. Authorities accessed phone's GPS and WiFi. Attached image designates geolocation.

Pulling up the attached image, Merlin saw the longitude and latitude crosshairs over a location.

Harrison Square.

Ethan Long's place.

The man who had served a five-year sentence in the Georgia State Prison for possessing a dangerous weapon; namely a *recoilless rifle* capable of firing explosive or non-explosive rockets. How could he have been so stupid to have missed it? He had the report, right?

Merlin set the phone down and put the pickup in drive. He stamped down on the gas, leaving a black streak of anger on the asphalt. People could die because of his stupidity.

As he drove, he wondered just how deep Long was involved in this thing. He had assumed the man they called 'Blackie', the man with the muscles on his muscles, Micah Blackledge, was the leader. Had Long played him? He was determined to find out but in the end, it didn't matter. No matter who led, whatever plan they had needed to be stopped. Period.

MERLIN PARKED IN THE same visitor's lot in Harrison Square as before and got out. Stopping in the street and storming inside Long's place didn't make sense since he was only one man and he had no idea how many might be in the two room apartment. Or how well armed they were. A surgical strike made more sense. It also offered retreat, if necessary. An idea he hated to even think about but it was there as a possibility. With the Beretta in the conceal carry holster in the back of his jeans, Merlin headed toward Long's place cautiously. The man's truck was sitting in front of his place. And just like before, the surrounding street was empty and quiet.

With his senses on high alert, Merlin kept an eye on the front door as he walked along the sidewalk to the back of the pickup.

Giving the street and the surrounding buildings one last check, he then slipped along the side of the truck and pulled the Beretta, holding it discreetly along the side of his leg. He couldn't afford to have someone on Neighborhood Watch see him and call out 'gun' in warning.

No one seemed to be watching so he hustled quickly to the door, brought the Beretta up to his waist and reached for the door knob. Merlin froze on the spot–

The door was open a crack.

There was a metallic, sulphur-like scent in the air

Someone had fired a weapon inside.

Merlin brought the Beretta up and holding it with both hands he bumped the door open with his shoulder and slid inside, sweeping the room. It was empty. He tread lightly across the floor to the small bedroom. The smell was heavier here– Merlin could see why. A body was on its knees and slumped over beside a cot. He moved in and checked for a pulse. Nothing. Looking closer, he saw it was Ethan Long. There was blood on his lip like he had been punched. But that wasn't what had killed him. He had been shot twice. A double tap in the back of the head, execution style.

Merlin let out a sharp breath and stood up. Another dead end.

He stood still, trying to make sense of what had happened here. The troopers had called this location. That he knew. He bent down and searched the body. No cell phone. He looked around. The 'bedroom' held the single cot and a small dresser. He checked it and found nothing other than a few pairs of socks and underwear.

Moving back into the other room, Merlin could see a table and two chairs, a hotplate, a small fridge that held little and several cupboards that he checked. They held some boxes of cereal, sugar, coffee and little else. One thing was sure, beyond the luxurious truck,

Ethan Long hadn't owned very much. And there was no sign of any cell phone.

Theory; Ethan Long had received the phone call. He had let Micah Blackledge know. Or Blackledge was here at the time. Either way, Blackledge was angry that the man Ethan had brought to the group was following the truck with the Davy Crockett. And Long's source may have come back with information on the Kleavon Watkins 'shooting' as well, revealing the truth. The execution followed, maybe after an interrogation, but Long wouldn't have any answers.

All nice and neat and it explained everything.

Except for how Merlin was going to find the Davy Crockett and the six Atomic warheads.

Chapter 32

MERLIN SLIPPED THE BERETTA back into the holster and stepped outside, closing the door to keep anyone from just walking in on the crime scene. As if he hadn't already compromised it. But that was the least of his worries right now. He ran a hand through his hair, trying to figure out what to do next. He supposed retrieving his cell phone and contacting the local PD was next up. Or should that be the FBI?

He rubbed the stubble on his face as he stepped away from the door, a reminder he hadn't slept, shaved or showered in some time— he looked at Long's truck...the Ford F-250 Super Duty pickup and something rattled around in his brain. He just couldn't put a finger on it. He walked to the driver-side window and looked in. Maybe he should search it? He glanced over at the front door, thinking. He'd searched his body but Long didn't have the keys on him. He started back to see if it was on a hook he'd missed or was in a drawer— he stopped again and rubbed the back of his neck. There was something about the truck that nagged at him. After a moment of thought, a vague memory came back to him and he turned and walked to the back of the truck, thinking about it.

That second night in the Chattahoochee Roadhouse parking lot he had watched Brianna Long pass a thick, brown envelope to Ethan. He had wondered then what was in it. But he had also wondered what Ethan had done with it. The sticker in the window had sidetracked him that night when he had started to look. He couldn't afford to be sidetracked now.

He remembered seeing a flash of light on the tailgate and Merlin now stood with his hands on the back end of the truck, looking for an answer. Everything looked like a normal tailgate and truck bed...but...Ethan Long had excelled at bodywork at the Georgia State Prison. That's what they had said. If anyone could do it, Long could...or could have since he was dead. Merlin shook his head at his self-correcting tendencies, even with all that was happening. His fingers moved along the smooth metal, warm from the sun already, looking for an answer. Nothing stood out. He lowered the tailgate and checked the inside surface. Nothing out of the ordinary. He ran his hands over the truck bed. It was lined with a custom, thermoplastic material without any seams that he could see. He lifted the tailgate back up in place and took a step away, thinking about what exactly he saw that night.

Long had bent over first, *then* lowered the tailgate–

Merlin squatted, running his hands along the underside of the tailgate, feeling for something. Anything. He shifted to his left. Then to the right. No, there was nothing out of the ordinary– wait. Merlin moved his hands back over the surface underneath. It felt like a circle, like a button in the metal surface. He pressed on it but didn't feel any movement. He pressed firmer and it sunk a quarter inch and he felt more than heard vibrations on both sides of the tailgate. But as he squatted there, nothing looked different. He thought back to that night. Long had bent over...pressing the button...then he–

Merlin stood up quickly and lowered the tailgate. But this time the tailgate was locked into the lower portion of the back-end and a one-foot section appeared below the level of the truck bed. There were two drawers built into the truck bed. Merlin bent forward and pulled open the right one. It slid out smoothly and he saw a Colt 9mm SMG submachine gun laying inside, a weapon used by the United States Marine Corps, the U.S. Marshals Service and some other law enforcement organizations. In the United States, felons are not legally allowed to bear arms. And Ethan Long was a felon. But Long was dead and this wasn't a recoilless rifle. And definitely not the Davy Crockett, which was more important at the moment.

Merlin closed the long drawer and slid open the one on the left. A large, hand-stitched leather satchel lay inside. He grabbed the strap and pulled it out. He was surprised at how heavy it felt. Merlin set it on the lowered tailgate, undid the two buckles and opened the flap. The satchel held a thick wad of papers that he pulled out and looked through. At first, he wasn't sure what they were. And then it dawned on him. These were parts of court transcripts, police reports, federal wiretap reports, emails between agencies...in short, these guys knew who was being monitored or investigated and almost every federal agent, police officer and many of the state and federal undercover operatives. He wondered if the undercover detectives who had helped him were in here? It didn't matter. He didn't have time for anything beyond the atomic weapons. But the contents of the envelope meant they had inside help. No doubt this Rylee McDonald that he had seen here helping Ethan Long was involved since she worked at the Federal Courthouse– he spotted the name of Morgan Walker as the court stenographer on one of the documents. Then another.

Merlin closed his eyes, thinking back to his reports. Rylee Mc-Donald was working as a law clerk at the local federal courthouse. Morgan Walker was a court reporter there. Chloe Green...she was working in a law office in Gainesville and....Brianna Long worked in the Gainesville Municipal Court. It all made sense. They had inside, confidential information on lawyers, judges and who knows what else. *That* was what Brianna had passed to her brother, parts of court documents that would have been heavily redacted if a member of the public had gotten them through a freedom of information request.

This gave him something he could work with. He could start with Morgan Walker and use what he found as a lever.

He put everything back into the satchel and threw the strap over his shoulder. Closing the drawer and the tailgate, he then hustled back to this own truck. Once there, he sent a text message to Laurent, outlining exactly what he needed to strengthen his leverage over Morgan Walker. Then he slammed the truck in drive and headed for Walker's apartment.

Chapter 33

REGENT LANDING APARTMENTS on Regent Court was a two-tone, brown-brick building that had seen better days. Merlin parked just down the street in case her militia friends were with her and he wanted the element of surprise on his side. He moved swiftly to the front entrance, carrying the heavy satchel over his shoulder, keeping his head down and ready to pull his weapon as soon as necessary. The building inside smelled like someone had just painted the walls but there was also a slight musty odor from somewhere. Merlin pushed these secondary thoughts to the back of his mind. He wasn't here to rent.

Walker's apartment was Number One and he moved to the door with the small one on it and leaned his ear against the door. There was the low sound of a television playing and that was it. Pulling the Beretta, Merlin knocked on the door, placed the weapon behind his thigh and stood a foot away and to the side.

It took a moment for the door to swing open and the tall redhead appeared. Her normal audacious attitude instantly changed to one of annoyance, "*What* do you want?"

Merlin took a step, trying discreetly to see if anyone was inside. He didn't need her to alert anyone who might be with her, "I just need to talk–"

The door started swinging closed, "Not interested—"

He moved forward quickly, putting a hand out to stop the door and swinging the weapon up, pointing it directly between her eyes. "I'm not asking," he said in a low voice. He scanned the living room for signs of anyone else, "Are you alone?"

Morgan Walker's hands were up as she backed away and her mouth moved but no words came out.

Merlin slipped inside and kicked the door shut with his heel, sweeping the room with the Beretta, "Answer me."

She moved back a few more feet, hands up but mute.

Dropping the satchel on a glass coffee table, Merlin gestured to a worn couch, "Sit down. Now."

Morgan's mouth moved a couple of times and then she moved over and sat with a soft thud.

Merlin moved to an open doorway. It was a small kitchen area, littered with dishes but empty of anyone. There was a small hallway to the left and he gestured to it, "What's down there?"

The redhead licked her lips and tried to talk but her mouth was dry.

"Is there anyone down there?"

Morgan shook her head, her voice shaky, "No. No. It's a bathroom and...my bedroom...." She looked stricken as the last word came out of her mouth.

Moving back to her, Merlin said, "Don't worry, I'm not here for anything like that. I just need to know what your Coal Mountain Militia friends are planning."

Her brow furrowed and she shook her head, "I don't know what you're talking about. What do you mean...planning...?"

There were some books on the glass coffee table and Merlin swept them off with the back of his hand.

Morgan watched the books tumble to the floor with a crash, "Hey!"

Undoing the two buckles, Merlin opened the flap and tipped the satchel, spilling the contents across the table, "You're involved in this up to your eyeballs, Walker."

Blinking at what she saw, Morgan slowly reached forward.

Merlin had put the two documents with her name on top of the stack of papers when he had returned everything to the satchel and he watched her reaction. He heard a car door shut outside the small picture window and he kept an eye on Morgan as he slid across the room to move aside the sheers to see who was out front.

Morgan ran her finger along the bottom of a page, "This URL shows it came from my system at work. Where...where did you get these? *How* did you get these?"

"Don't play dumb. You know exactly where they came from," Merlin said as he headed back across the room for the front door, "Your friend Ethan Long thought they'd never be found, but he was wrong."

"Ethan?"

"Like I said, don't play dumb. You and your friends are facing Federal time. If you come clean and help me, maybe I can help with how much time you get." Merlin had no idea if he had any influence but it was worth a gamble to get her to cooperate.

A moment later, Morgan looked over at him, her brows knit together, "Who the hell are you? And why should I trust you? I know Ethan but I don't know you at all." She sat back, waving her arms, "I'm not saying anything. As far as I'm concerned, this is all some con game and you're trying to play me."

"Suit yourself," Merlin said as he opened the door and walked back toward her.

A moment later, two men appeared at the open door.

Merlin gave them a wave, "Come on in, gentlemen. Close the door and please show Morgan Grace Walker here who you are."

Morgan blinked, "How the hell do you know my middle name? I never...."

The two stepped inside, looking unsure but each digging under their black hoodie sweatshirt and pulling out a badge on a chain around their neck.

"I'm Detective Xavier Grummett, Gainesville PD."

"Detective Kaleb Jones, Gainesville Police Department." He closed the door behind them.

Morgan's face had a look of apprehension on it now as she looked at the two detectives.

Merlin gestured to the papers on the desk, "Morgan here has been helping the Coal Mountain Militia get access to court papers. None of those papers on the table were obtained through the Freedom of Information Act. The FOIA exemptions would have made sure the sensitive information on them was redacted. I found them in Ethan Long's truck and thanks to her, they have a good handle on all the local and federal undercover operatives."

The two detectives looked at each other and then walked over to look at the papers on the glass coffee table.

Merlin watched Morgan push her hands into her hair, looking desperate, and he wondered if she would cave. If not, he would have to find another way to find the Davy Crockett and the atomic projectiles. And he wasn't sure if he had another way that would be fast enough to stop whatever was in store for the country.

Chapter 34

GRUMMETT AND JONES were bent over the papers, looking through them as Merlin watched. Grummett cursed softly under his breath, "Do you think we're in here? I mean...this could be bad...."

"Yeah," Jones agreed, "I've already seen three of the local feds I know." He shook his head somberly as he straightened up with several papers in his hands, "And these are...this doesn't look good. Miss Morgan, if you want to help yourself–"

"Look, look, look," Morgan said as she shot forward on the couch, "I don't have anything to do with any of this. I don't care what Caleb...or whatever the hell his name is...I didn't give these to Ethan Long, no matter what he says."

Grummett gestured to her with the papers in his hand, "These have *your* name on them–"

"I know that. But I didn't give them to Ethan. Someone else must have given them to him." She glared at Merlin, "*If* he had them. I don't trust that son of a bitch. Go and ask him yourself instead of listening to this b.s.–

"They can't ask him," Merlin said.

"And why the hell not," Morgan yelled.

"Because he's dead." Merlin made a gun gesture with his hand, "Someone put two in the back of his head, execution-style."

Morgan was stunned, tears forming in her eyes.

The two detectives were equally stunned as they looked at Merlin.

"I found him in his bedroom, kneeling over next to the small bed he had," Merlin explained. "I found those papers and a Colt 9mm SMG submachine gun when I searched his truck. He had two secret drawers accessed by the tailgate. "

Grummett looked at his partner, his voice quiet as he said, "This is starting to get real serious. I guess we should call it in."

Jones nodded slowly as he glanced at the papers in his hand, "Yeah. I guess we should. And I guess it's up to the District Attorney on what happens with her about these–"

Morgan Walker shot forward on the sofa, pushing the pile of papers around, "No, no, no. You got it all wrong." She grabbed several from the pile and set them down, flipping them around to show the two detectives, "Look. These ones are from Judge Otis G. McDaniel. I don't work for him. I don't have access to *any* of his stuff. And this one is from Judge Portiere. I can't get any of this stuff. Check at the courthouse and they'll tell you that. I don't have access to any of these."

Jones picked up one of the papers, looking at it, "Okay. Then who does?"

"The only person who could get those are–" Morgan suddenly shut up, her eyes blinking. She sat back, crossing her arms over her chest.

Grummett glanced at Merlin and then at the redhead, "Either you're involved in getting these papers or someone is setting you up. This is going to result in a lot of jail time–"

Merlin interrupted him, "Actually, it will probably involve time at the Guantanamo Bay detention camp in some black hole. We're talking terrorism here."

Morgan looked confused, "What are you talking about? I don't have anything to do with those papers and I have even less to do with terrorism."

Grummett and Jones both looked confused as well. "No offense, pal, but I'm a little lost here," Jones said.

"Yeah, I'm with Jonesy," Grummett said as he stood up. "What *are* we talking about?"

Merlin wasn't sure exactly how much he should reveal but he knew he had to open up enough to give them enough information to understand the full situation. He wondered if Laurent would take him out to the woods and shoot him. He took a breath and told them, "I was sent to look into the Coal Mountain Militia running guns up the Iron Pipeline."

"We got a lot of guys running guns up I-95," Jones said. "Why these guys?"

"Let's just say there were suspicions of them planning something. What it was, we weren't sure."

"Okay," Grummett said, looking at him to add more than that.

"And no, I'm not going to say who I work for. But what I can tell you is I tracked a shipment of guns from Atlanta to Gainesville and up to New York. The Feds are taking care of both ends for now. But I ended up trailing a vehicle back here. It turns out that panel truck I followed was carrying a Davey Crockett, a recoilless rifle from the 1950s that was stolen from the U.S. Army Ordnance Museum in Fort Lee approximately two weeks ago."

"So they're dealing in antique weapons as well. Big deal," Jones said. "I know it's a federal crime, but what does that have to do with terrorism?"

Grummett shook his head, "No. The 50s wouldn't be antique. It has to be at least 100 years old."

Jones held his hands out, "So what? It's still not terrorism—"

"It is if they're going to use it in an attack on American soil," Merlin said.

Grummett looked at Merlin with skepticism, "Why would they use a weapon from the 50s? Are they trying to sneak into some art museum or—"

"My sources tell me the Coal Mountain Militia might have six projectiles used in the Davy Crockett rifle. They were supposed to have been destroyed but an old General kept them under lock and key. They disappeared after he died."

"Okay," Jones said, "and...?"

"The Davy Crockett used an M-388 round that utilized a version of the Mk-54 warhead," Merlin explained. He looked at Morgan, "They're 20-ton Atomic bombs."

Chapter 35

THERE WAS TOTAL SILENCE in the apartment as Grummett and Jones exchanged shocked looks. It was Grummett who finally spoke, his voice tight as he asked Merlin, "Did you say...Atomic...bombs?"

"Yeah."

The two detectives looked at each other again, finding it hard to believe. But then they both looked at Morgan.

Put on the spot, she looked positively scared, "I...I don't know anything about...no Atomic bombs. Why would you think–"

"Because my intelligence pinpointed their last call to Ethan Long's place," Merlin said. "Which is where I found those court records, as I said. And they point to you. All the evidence says you're up to your neck in it."

The two detectives exchanged looks over the use of the word 'intelligence' but didn't say anything.

Morgan shook her head emphatically, "No. I don't care what you say. I already told you, I didn't have anything to do with those papers and I don't have anything to do with any bombs."

Grummett took a deep breath, stared at Morgan for a moment and then said, "What he says is right, Miss Morgan. Everything points to you being mixed up in this whole thing. The chain of evidence points right at *you*."

"Unless you can give us a reason to think you're *not* involved," Jones offered.

She finally caved, "Okay, okay, okay. It has to be Rylee McDonald. She's the one works for Judge McDaniel. And she fills in for others, like Judge Portiere. I swear." Morgan sat back, crossing her arms over her chest, "She's the only one who could have done it. And the bitch set me up for it."

Grummett and Jones looked to Merlin for confirmation of the name.

He nodded, "It's entirely possible. But we'd have to prove that wouldn't we, Morgan?"

"Why are you asking me?"

"Because you're on the hook if we can't. Doesn't she live in this building?"

There was a moment of silence. "Yes. She lives across the– you're not expecting me–? How am I supposed to–?"

"Is she home? Get her over here."

Morgan sat afraid and unsure for a moment.

Merlin looked at Grummett and Jones, who both looked unsure themselves, and he said, "If we go over there and knock, she could refuse to let us in. And she runs or lets the others know. But if she comes over here, we can gang up on her."

Jumping up from the sofa, Morgan headed for the door, "*That* sounds good to me. I don't want to be on the hot seat any longer–"

Merlin reached out and caught her elbow, "Keep in mind you're still on the hot seat if this doesn't work."

Morgan pulled her arm away and snarled, "Fine. Whatever I saw in you...." She moved to the door, pulled it open and strode across the hall and knocked.

Grummett was looking at Merlin, one eyebrow raised.

Merlin shrugged, "Comes with the job. I learned that from James Bond."

"Books or movies?" Jones asked.

"I like the books better," Grummett said. He turned his head from Merlin when voices sounded in the hall.

A moment later, Morgan came walking briskly back into the apartment and marched over to the glass coffee table.

Rylee McDonald came walking in behind her, stopping in surprise when she saw the three men. Then her eyes narrowed as she looked at Merlin.

Jones shut the door behind her.

McDonald looked at the closed door for a moment and then at Merlin, wondering what was happening.

Morgan pointed down at the papers strewn across the coffee table, her voice harsh, "Don't look at him, bitch. Look here. *You* took those from the courthouse, didn't you? And you tried to frame me for it."

McDonald took her eyes off Merlin and looked at the papers, shaking her head for a moment until she recognized what they were. Her manner changed and she crossed her arms, giving a slight shrug, "I don't know what you're talking about."

"We found *your* prints all over them," Grummett said, "every single one."

McDonald turned her head at him, her attitude defiant, "What are you talking about? And who the hell are you anyway?"

Grummett held up the badge on the chain around his neck, "Detective Xavier Grummett, Gainesville PD. That's my partner, Detective Jones."

Her manner changed again, this time to one of fear. She licked her lips, "I...."

Jones finished her sentence, "Will spend time in jail if you don't cooperate."

Her foot began to tap as she tightened her arms over her chest and she seemed torn between staying quiet and opening up.

They just waited.

Her voice was just a whisper, "I had no choice."

"What do you mean?" Jones asked. "You *always* have a choice—"

"No, I didn't. Not really." McDonald chewed on her lower lip and then said, "I was forced into it. I was picked up by State Troopers with...with some drugs in my car. They weren't mine, I'm sure someone planted them but...it didn't matter. I was told it would all go away...if I was willing to help—"

"Told by who?" Grummett asked.

"He'll kill me if I say."

"We can protect you."

"No one can protect me from him," she countered.

"Think of Madison," Merlin said.

The mention of her little girl caught McDonald by surprise.

Merlin glanced at the two detectives, "I'm sure we can put you both in witness protection. As long as you cooperate like Morgan did."

Grummett nodded as she looked at him.

McDonald still looked unsure, "I don't know. I want to...but...who would believe State Troopers would be involved in the whole thing—?"

"I do," Merlin interjected. He stepped forward, "I was stopped by two State Troopers not long ago and they stuck me in a trunk. They took me to a secluded location and I'd probably be buried in some shallow grave if I hadn't been able to fight back. I had to kill one of them." He glanced at Grummett and Jones who had shocked expression, "The FBI was called in and took over that part of the case."

"You have to talk, Rylee," Morgan urged, "they have Atomic bombs they're going to use."

"What?" McDonald shook her head, her eyes wide with shock, "No way. No way. I don't know anything about–" Her head dipped suddenly and her eyes looked back and forth in panic.

Merlin moved closer, angling his head to look at her, "What is it? You know something. What is it?"

Chapter 36

RYLEE'S EYES KEPT DARTING as she looked down at the floor, her mind obviously trying to process something, "It was...all Blackie's idea...."

"Micah Blackledge?"

"Y-yeah. He's the one who told me he would take care of the troopers...if I got him information from the courthouse. I passed it to Brianna Long who passed it to Ethan. That way Blackie was never directly involved. Anyway...I had no choice...."

To Merlin, it had the ring of truth to it and he told the two detectives, "I saw Brianna passing a thick envelope to her brother."

The two detectives mulled over the information.

"Yeah. And I'm pretty sure Brianna was set up, too," Rylee added. "I don't think she ever told her brother but she added stuff from the Gainesville Municipal Court where she worked."

"That makes sense," Merlin said. "What else can you tell us?"

She opened her mouth but closed it again, looking apprehensive as she rubbed the back of her neck

"Rylee?" He waited a moment and then Merlin said, "Keep in mind, if anything happens, all bets and witness protection are off."

She cleared her throat, her voice barely audible as she said something.

"Can you speak up?" Jones asked.

Clearing her throat again and clearly shaken, Rylee said, "Blackie came to see me this morning?"

That surprised Merlin, "He did?" Maybe it wasn't Blackledge who killed Long.

"Yeah. And he was pissed. On a real high, kind of. I don't know how to explain it."

"When was this?" Jones asked, being very much the detective in the questioning.

"Real early. Like 5:30. Like I say, he was real jumpy and upset and–"

"What did he want?" interjected Grummett, pushing her along in her story.

Rylee shrugged, like she was reluctant to say and then, "He wanted a phone number. I was really surprised because...it was unusual–"

"Why?"

She shrugged a shoulder again, tightening her arms around herself, "Because normally it was Ethan Long who talked to me, who did that stuff. Blackie always stayed away from getting involved directly. I'm not sure why Ethan didn't do it this time–?"

"Because he's dead," Morgan blurted out.

That shocked Rylee and she immediately put her hands together over face steeple-like, "Oh no. Oh no. I thought he had blood on him and...."

That did it for Merlin. He was right. It was Micah Blackledge who had killed Long. And it sounded like he was getting–

Rylee put her hands up and backed away a step, "I can't do this. I can't. He'll kill me, too. And Madison." She shook her head, "No, no, no."

Morgan got up and went to her, wrapping her arms around her, "I'm sorry. I didn't mean to..."

The two women hugged each other, tears flowing.

Merlin spoke up, "I'm sorry, ladies, but keep in mind we're trying to find six Atomic weapons. When I mentioned them earlier, Rylee, it struck a nerve. Now, *why* did Blackie want this number?"

Morgan whispered to her, "You have to tell them what you know. It's the only way we can get out of this. Otherwise...."

Rylee nodded after a moment. She stepped out of Morgan's comforting embrace and wiped tears from her eyes, "I don't know if it means anything...but...Blackie was talking to this guy out of New York before–"

"New York? How did they meet?" Grummett asked.

She shrugged again, "I'm not sure. But...they called him raghead...." She glanced around, "You know....cause he's...he was born here....but he calls himself an Arab and...."

"How is it *you* know this guy?" Jones asked. "Did you introduce them to each other?" His voice was harsh, accusative.

"No. I didn't. I don't know how they met. I only know about it because...Blackie came to me...I had some contacts through my job from several seminars I was on and...he had me check to see if this guy was on anyone's radar." She glanced at the two detectives, "The police, I mean. I didn't have a choice–"

"Fine," Jones said, "we understand. Get to the meat of it."

Blackie said he was going to do a big gun deal...the guy was going to pay a *lot* of money. No...no...he said a big *weapons* deal...I remember those words because he never said it that way before...you know?"

"Yeah," Merlin said, rolling his hand for her to get to the meat as Jones said.

She swallowed, "He...Blackie...he called the guy as he was leaving my place...which surprised me. He was in a real hurry and I heard him say...bring the money...all six mill."

"Six mill? As in six *million* dollars?" Jones asked.

Merlin didn't care about the money and he rolled his hand to keep her talking, sure he was going to find out where the warheads were, "Bring it where?"

Rylee took her eyes from Jones and turned them to Merlin, "Blackie told him... to go out to the compound. In Coal Mountain, you know...?"

"Yeah. What else?"

"That's all I know. Except the guy's name was Husain Assaff." She spelled it and said, "Double a and double f. He insisted on that for some reason. Like he was going to make a name for himself or something like that."

Merlin and the two detectives looked at each other for a moment.

"I never heard of this guy," Jones said.

Grummett shook his head, "No, me neither." He shrugged, "Maybe the Feds have him on their radar and we can let them know."

"I'm not sure we have the time for them to investigate," Merlin said.

Jones had a sour look on his face, "I can't believe a guy would want to help someone attack his own country. Or help some...outsider...to do it."

"You have to understand Blackie," Rylee said as she rubbed the back of her neck. "He's a bitter guy. He had some old uncles who came back from Vietnam years ago who were broken from the war and they all said the government never did anything to help them.

And he had some cousins who went through the same thing in Iraq and Afghanistan–"

"That doesn't make it right," Jones snapped.

Rylee swallowed as she rubbed at the tension, "I'm just saying...."

"What matters right now is stopping it," Merlin said. "Rylee? Do you know where these 'weapons' they were selling to this Assaff...double a and double f...would be kept inside the compound?"

Rylee shrugged her shoulders again, "Not really. I heard Blackie say he would take the guy into the back of the ammunitions depot but I have no idea what that is–"

"That's what they call the last Quonset hut in the compound," interjected Morgan. It was her turn to shrug as everyone looked at her, "I was there in the compound a couple of times when Gavin was showing off and he took me there to shoot guns. That's where they keep all their ammunition and stuff. They can even make their own bullets there. If that matters." Her voice trailed off.

Merlin looked to the two detectives.

It was Grummett who shook his head, "No. I'm not sure we could get a warrant to go in and take a look. Me and Jones have had more than this and had problems."

"He's right," Jones said in agreement. "And I don't think we've ever crossed paths personally with this Micah Blackledge, so we've got no paperwork to use as a basis."

"No, I don't think so either," Grummett said. "And even if we try to get a warrant based on what the ladies here have said, the lawyers would probably call it hearsay or some other b.s."

Jones looked at Merlin, "And before you say *just try*, keep in mind it's out of our jurisdiction as well. We don't have any relationship with the legal beagles there."

Grummett shook his head and had a look of distaste on his face, "And to make it even worse, Coal Mountain is in Forsyth County, which is Post 44...the State Troopers have jurisdiction there."

Jones swore, "Yeah. And considering the story about a couple of troopers in this thing, we have no idea...." He gave Merlin a quizzical look and then asked him, "What about you? You seem to have a lot of pull?"

Merlin felt his jaw tighten. It was back to him again. And he always seemed to be one step behind of these guys and now...a moment later, he looked at Grummett, "You have a card with a cell phone number where I can call you or send you a text?"

Grummett pulled several business cards from his pocket, thumbed through them and handed one over, "You can use that one. What are you going to do?"

"Better you don't know. I'll be in touch."

Chapter 37

MERLIN DRAGON WAS tired and irritable. This had to end *now*. Back in his pickup truck, he pulled out his cell phone and did a search based around a tentative plan that was forming in the back of his mind. It was a long shot and a bit stupid but– he found a possibility on the far edge of town and called up Google maps to get an overhead view. Everything looked promising and more. Checking the local news, it appeared everything would be a go right now and he wouldn't have to wait until the middle of the night. He did another search and found a place where he could get what he needed to do the job. Setting the phone in the cup holder, he headed across town, bought a 48 inch, heavy duty bolt cutter and then headed directly for his target.

Parking across from the fenced-in perimeter of a U.S. Army Reserve Armored Training Center, Merlin looked for guards. But everything at the large red-brick building was quiet and he didn't see any personnel patrolling the grounds behind it. Which was expected since the local news said the reserve unit had been taken to Fort Bragg, North Carolina for training. He drove to the side street where a new building was being constructed opposite the Center and he parked just beyond it.

Getting out with the bolt cutter in hand and standing by the truck for a moment, Merlin checked his surroundings. The building site was quiet and the small warehouse just ahead was quiet as well. Everything still looked like a go. He kept the bolt cutter against his side as he moved across the street to the ten-foot high, chain link fence. Working quickly, Merlin cut a six-foot high slice in the fence and squeezed through. He set the tool on the grass and then made sure the fence looked as normal as possible from the street. Then he turned and set to his task, hustling across to the line of vehicles behind the building. Most of them were light utility vehicles for carrying personnel, ranging from jeep-size to Humvee-size.

At the very back was a vehicle he could use. It was a Stryker, an eight-wheeled, armored fighting vehicle. He clambered onboard and checked inside. But it didn't take long for his hopes to be crushed. This was a basic training vehicle and had been stripped of what he needed. It was also possible it was being upgraded but it didn't matter. It wouldn't work. He climbed out and jumped to the ground. He checked a few more prospects but was almost ready to give up when he spotted the back end of a vehicle behind a maintenance shack. He sprinted across the gravel and came to a stop on the other side of the shack.

It was a four-wheeled M1117 Guardian Armored Security Vehicle, also known as a Commando. Unlike the Stryker, this Commando had a bank of four electrically operated smoke grenade launchers, mounted either side of the turret, a 90 mm low-pressure cannon mounted on the turret and an M240H Medium machine gun mounted outside the gunner's hatch. The side doors were locked so he clambered up and entered through the roof hatch to check it out. Sitting in the main seat behind the steering wheel,

Merlin surveyed the olive-drab interior. He realized this was actually better than he had hoped. It was an advanced model that had everything you could want; a laser designator and rangefinder, thermal imager, digital command and control system, a blended inertial/global positioning system navigation, targeting capability and more. And best of all, it was equipped with a control system that allowed everything to be done from the inside. There were even several firing ports, holes in the armor to fire personal weapons through.

The 260 hp Cummins engine started with a growl and the slight smell of industrial diesel filled the interior. Merlin carefully steered the 30,000 lb vehicle around the shack and toward the hole he had cut in the fence. He had no plans to smash through. Instead, he wanted to keep his 'borrowing' the vehicle as quiet as possible. Getting closer to the ten-foot high fence, he could see his truck through the ballistic glass and it was still the only vehicle on the side street. So far, so good.

Stopping inside the fence, Merlin got out, squeezed through the opening and ran for his pickup. He grabbed his cell phone because he would need it and his weapon. Driving the truck back to the main street, he left it parked under a tree just beyond two other parked trucks and then sprinted back.

Once inside the fence again, he used the bolt cutters to create a large, three-sided cut-out, leaving one side intact to serve as a hinge. It was tough working up higher to get enough room for the eight-and-half foot tall vehicle through but his anger at the whole situation pushed him. He pulled the heavy fence away as much as possible and then used the Commando's bulk and power to push it through. Then he used the armored vehicle to push the section back in place and used the cutters to cut some pieces to tie the sec-

tion back together. It was make-shift but would hide the fact someone had cut through, at least from the street.

The sound of the Cummins engine bounced lightly off the
buildings he passed as Merlin kept his speed down, trying to keep
anyone from noticing him in the Commando. As if. A few kids
shouted in delight as he passed and they took up the chase. He
took it up to forty mph and left them behind. Ten minutes later,
he was on the highway and took it up to seventy. It was nerve rack-
ing, passing cars with startled drivers and passengers and wondering how soon state troopers might show up. But he had no choice.
Once he got across the long stretch of Brown's Bridge, he could go
cross-country, evading 'capture' if needed. The Commando was capable of fording 5-foot depths of water, climbing gradients of 60%,
negotiating 30% side slope, overcoming obstacles of five feet and
had a foot-and-a-half ground clearance. He would do whatever was
necessary.

But no one stopped him. Finally reaching a back road on the
far side of his target, Merlin prepared for his assault.

Chapter 38

MERLIN PARKED ON the edge of the back road, outside the chain-link perimeter fence of the Coal Mountain Militia Compound. He was on the opposite side from the rolling gate he had first encountered. He had no intention of going in through the front door.

The first thing he did was find the video he had shot flying over the compound with the drone. He had the idea on the drive here but he had no idea if this would work. But it was worth a try. If not, he would simply use the old-fashioned method, his eyes. A USB male to Lightning male cable was already plugged into one of the data ports on the Commando's DAGR system and Merlin hooked it up to his phone. The DAGR or Defense Advanced GPS Receiver was supposed to allow you to load map sets and enhance your situational awareness by enabling you to display the maps and set waypoints, routes and alerts on its moving map display. It took a few minutes to figure it out, but it seemed to load the video. Unplugging the phone, Merlin accessed the map display. It worked! The system had accepted the data/map transfer and he had a tactical overhead view and the coordinates of every square inch inside the compound. It was time to go.

He had chosen to park near a spot with a gap in the trees between the road and the fence and Merlin now reversed the Commando and backed up, turning on the road to face that gap. Gunning the big diesel engine, he gripped the steering, readied himself and then stomped down on the accelerator.

The Commando shot across the grass and between the trees, slamming into and through the perimeter fence. There was no doubt the intrusion sensors would be sounding the alarm. But the jackasses had no idea what was coming.

INSIDE A ROOM IN THE large, two-story building in the compound, a man stood in front of a floor to ceiling window casually drinking a cup of coffee. He was dressed in combat boots and a camouflage military uniform with the Coal Mountain Militia insignia patch on the shoulder. He was watching a dozen of his comrades-in-arms entering one of the 40 ft × 100 ft Quonset huts. They were carrying cases of new ammunition for an upcoming training session—

Alarms sounded.

The man turned and looked at his security system. Not only were the alarms sounding but red lights were flashing on the board. Shaking his head, he walked across the wooden floorboards, "What the...?" He stood looking over the board and the flashing lights, sipping his coffee and thinking. Then he narrowed his eyes as he called out, "Hey, Blackie? You might wanna take a look at this."

It took a moment before the big man, dressed in camouflage fatigues as well, stepped into the room, irritated at the interruption, "What is it, Hawk? I've got to get the– what the...?"

"Exactly my words." Hawk gestured to the flashing lights, "I've never seen that many go off in one section. Maybe a tree fell on the fence?"

"Maybe."

A swarthy man with a thick, black beard stepped into the room behind Blackie, irritated at the ringing alarms, "What is the problem?" When he saw the lights flashing on the board, his face hardened, "You have an intrusion? I thought you said this was a secure place to do business–"

"It is," Blackie snapped. "Hawk, get Gonzo and Bigsby on their radio comms. They're out there working on the defensive training trenches. Have them check it out. If it's a tree, fine. But if it's an inquisitive local like we've had before, make them regret they disturbed us."

A macabre grin settled on Hawk's face as he walked over and reached for his VHF-UHF radio sitting on a desk, "I might even have them haul the joker in for a little face to face time for screwing up my day."

"Just get it done," Blackie said. He spun on his heels and gave the swarthy man a hard look, "Let's get back to business."

STATIC SOUNDED AND Gonzo Campbell, husky and muscular, pressed the blue A/B button on the left side of his Baofeng radio as he watched over the three dozen men, dressed in camouflage uniforms and working on the trenches. "Go ahead," he said into the radio.

"It's Hawk. We have something happening at the back of the perimeter. Alarms are going off and the lights are flashing like crazy in here. A whole section has gone off. Blackie wants you and Bigsby to check it out."

"Okay. Can do." Gonzo looked off at the woods that lay between this training area and the back fence, the smell of damp earth mingling with the slight smell of gun smoke from some recent firing practice.

"If some ass has come through, make him regret it. Out."

"That we can do for sure. Out." Gonzo picked up his Colt RO635 submachine gun leaning against a stump. It was a weapon normally used by the US Marine Corp and stolen from a shipment before it ever reached the unit it was destined for. "Bigsby," he called out, "we got a job."

Allen Bigsby was a tall, strapping white guy with a large, blue tattoo in place of his head hair. Bigsby had grown up training in this compound from the time he could walk and he climbed up the side of a trench without question, his own favorite weapon in hand, a Heckler & Koch MP7A1 submachine gun normally used by US Navy Seals.

Gonzo climbed into a Storm Search and Rescue Tactical Vehicle used by the U.S. Armed Forces and stowed his rifle between the seats.

Bigsby opened the passenger side door and ducked his head under the flat roof as he climbed inside. He cradled his weapon as he pulled the door shut with a bang, "What are we doing?"

"Checking out the rear perimeter fence for Blackie. Hawk says his alarms are going off." He put the vehicle in gear, the 430 hp engine growled and the 4,300 lb vehicle headed for the trees.

Setting the butt of his weapon on his thigh, Bigsby looked eager, "Hope we find someone this time."

Gonzo emitted a grunt of agreement.

Chapter 39

MERLIN STEERED THE massive, sand-colored, four-wheeled armored vehicle around a large oak tree, chewing up the ground as he climbed an incline. The heavy woods were slowing him down, giving the militia group time to react and he decided to take a more direct approach. As he came down the other side of the incline, he gunned the diesel engine and took on several smaller trees and bushes, rolling over and pushing his way through with a vengence. A twenty-foot wide stream appeared ahead but Merlin kept pushing the Commando down the steep bank. It was four feet deep but didn't slow the armored vehicle and water sliced away in huge sprays on either side. He made his way across and then climbed the bank on the other side. As the vehicle leveled out, Merlin saw an armored, jeep-like vehicle about one hundred and fifty yards away across a clearing, heading his way.

The brown-camouflage vehicle came to a stop.

Merlin slowed the Commando as the vehicle just sat there.

A moment later, two men jumped out and strode to the front of their jeep-like vehicle. Each carried a submachine gun and they brought them up to their shoulders and fired without hesitation.

The bullets pinged off the thick skin and the ballistic glass of the Commando.

Merlin activated the weapons system, flipped the hood off the trigger for the M240H Medium machine gun as he set the target and pressed the firing button. The heavy staccato of 950 rounds per minute filled the interior of the Commando

The two men stepped back as the bullets tore up the ground in front of them. When the firing ceased, the two men looked at each other, surprised they were still alive. Then one of them smiled and raised his weapon, opening up again.

Merlin cursed. They knew he was just trying to scare them, to send a message to 'get out of the way'. They saw through it. Fine. He changed his tactics. He accessed the targeting system and chose another weapon and a new target.

The two men stopped smiling as the 90 mm low-pressure cannon rotated five feet and lowered.

In their direction.

A moment later they jumped for cover.

Boom.

The heavy recoil of the cannon rocked the Commando.

The vehicle across the clearing exploded violently into flying, shredded tires and brown camouflage bits and pieces

Merlin stepped on the accelerator and moved across the clearing, his hand returning to the submachine gun and he alternated fire on either side of the burning hulk as pieces rained down on the two men hugging earth. They got the message and when he stopped firing, they scrambled to their feet and took off into the heavy woods in different directions.

INSIDE THE SECURITY room of the two-story building, Hawk stood at the window and coffee cup stopped halfway to his lips. He cocked his head, listening. He slowly turned his head, looking at the still flashing lights. He had shut off the annoying ringing alarms, assuming it was nothing. Or it was just some local teenagers interested in what lay beyond the wire fence. But the sound in the distance told him something different. Walking across to the board again, he set his coffee down and picked up his VHF-UHF radio, clicking the send button, "Gonzo?"

No answer.

"Gonzo? You there?"

Silence.

"Damn you, Gonzo. Stop screwing around."

Static filled the room and a frantic voice erupted with cursing and swearing then cut out.

Hawk looked at the radio and clicked the send button again, "What's going on? Gonzo? You there?"

The voice came back, frantic and breathing heavy, "Yeah, yeah. *They destroyed the Storm."*

"What are you talking about? Who is this they–?"

"How the hell do I know? All I know is they got armor with a machine gun and a cannon and a–"

Hawk shook his head, "Calm down, calm down, make sense." He cursed, "Put Bigsby on–"

"Screw you, Hawk. I don't even know where Bigsby is. Just get ready cause they're coming and they're pissed."

When the radio cut out again, Hawk looked at it like the man on the other side had two heads. Then he cleared his throat and called out, "Hey, Blackie? We may have a problem."

Chapter 40

THE MASSIVE COMMANDO shot from the trees and chewed up grass and dirt as it clawed its way across the open ground toward the training area dotted with foxholes and trenches. Through the ballistic glass, Merlin could see twenty to thirty men dressed in camouflage uniforms about two hundred yards away, many of them already hunkered down, only their heads and weapons showing. Three of the men were standing on the top of the trenches and they were pointing at him and yelling. A moment later, they jumped for cover.

The men in the foxholes and trenches opened up with withering automatic weapons fire.

Bullets pinged and ricocheted off the composite armor system and the ballistic glass of the Commando.

Merlin flipped the hood off the trigger for the M240H Medium machine gun again and opened up. He kept the heavy staccato up for a full minute, the 7.62×51 mm bullets tearing up the earth across the width of the training ground and back again.

As soon as he stopped firing, the men popped their heads up again and began peppering the Commando with everything they had.

It was time for a different tactic. Just beyond the foxholes and trenches were several military trucks. Using the laser designator to paint his target, Merlin fed the information to his range finder and let the system bring the 90 mm low-pressure cannon to bear.

Set, ready, fire.

Boom!

The shell landed dead center in an old M35 2½-ton cargo truck and it exploded violently. He fed his next target into the fire control system, pressed the trigger and a 5-ton, M939 military cargo truck exploded into twisted metal and shredded tires. It only took a moment to destroy a second M939 military truck.

The men in the trenches and the foxholes took the hint. They scrambled over the edges of their hiding places and scrambled in every direction. No one bothered to look back or try to lay down any more fire.

Merlin turned the Commando and chewed his way over the training ground, skirting the now-empty hiding holes and setting his target into the global positioning navigation system- the Quonset hut. That allowed him to watch for anyone trying to intercept him as he accelerated to 40 mph. And he knew more would try before he reached the huts in the far distance.

It only took a few more minutes before trucks and SUVs tore into the area in front of the two-story building and disgorged more armed men at the far side of the huts.

Merlin saw three men step out of the building itself. At one thousand yards, it was too far to be positive but he was sure Blackie would be one of them. Tough. He set the laser designator on a heavy duty truck and fed the information to the firing system for the 90mm cannon. He brought the big Commando to a stop and fired. The cannon boomed and the armored vehicle rocked.

The heavy-duty truck exploded in a ball of fire.

Merlin set the coordinates of a second truck as a target and fired.

It exploded and sent the men into chaos.

He chose a smaller jeep and fired.

The jeep did a complete twirl in the air as it exploded and disintegrated.

The men were undeterred and had taken up positions to fight from. Bullets began tearing up the ground around the Commando and began bouncing off the armor and ballistic glass. They were tossing lead at this distance in hopes of stopping his advance.

Time to send a bigger message.

Especially before they had time to break out some bigger weapons they might have.

Merlin targeted the two-story structure and blew a hole in the side, building materials flying everywhere. He adjusted the aim to the second floor and the shell tore through a window and exploded inside, sending flames licking out the broken window.

Next came the smoke grenade launchers. Merlin launched four 66mm smoke grenades and set down a line of smoke to hide his next move. He gunned the engine and was hitting 70 mph when he fired the next four smoke grenades. As he swung the Commando to the left, he accessed the M240H trigger again and lay down a line of machine gun fire into the smoke to the right to make them believe he was still coming at them.

Return gunfire started again as the men began firing blindly into the smoke.

As the side of the first Quonset hut appeared in the smoke, Merlin slowed and fired four more smoke grenades over the huts into the chaos of gunfire. And then four more along the back of the huts. Then he swung the Commando around the end of the hut to the back door. Dropping the Commando's side door, Merlin pulled the Beretta from the conceal carry holster and jumped out, checking the back door. It was locked. He didn't want to attract attention, even with all the gunfire still going on, so he pulled the bump key and went to work. It didn't take more than a few seconds and he was inside.

The hut smelled of gun oil and pistol powder. It was filled with rows of shelves holding bulk boxes of every type of ammunition you could imagine as well as large plastic jars of powder and numerous reloading kits. But that wasn't what he was here for. On the left were stacks of boxes filled with everything dealing with the process of bullet making, from bullet molds to bullet casting flux. He looked to his right and there they were. He recognized them from the pictures he had found in his search. But actually seeing them in plain sight, ten feet away on wooden pallets, was surreal. All six M-388 nuclear projectiles, each one two and a half feet long, eleven inches around and seventy-six pounds in weight, were sitting inside straw-filled wooden boxes. The tops of the wooden boxes lay on the floor, no doubt to showcase the goods to the buyer. There was no time to waste.

In the midst of the gunfire still sounding outside the hut, Merlin headed for the warheads.

A sound on the concrete floor caught his attention.

Merlin was half-turned when a large, snarling form shot from hiding behind the stack of bulk ammunition boxes and tackled him with a ferocity that nearly broke him in two. The Beretta clattered to the floor a moment before Merlin landed face down on the concrete, immense pain shooting through his body from the hard blow. Fog closed in over his eyes.

Chapter 41

MERLIN DRAGON FOUGHT the fog. This was a fight for his life as blows began landing down on the back of his head. Then large hands grabbed his hair and slammed his head into the concrete. The blow nearly made him black out but Merlin fought it.

The hands lifted his head for another blow–

A surprised angry voice suddenly sounded in his ear, "Rucker? I thought the troopers got you–? It doesn't matter. Whatever your name is, you're a dead man. No one interferes in my business."

Fear shot through Merlin's body as he tried to regain the breath knocked from his lungs. He recognized the voice; Micah Blackledge. And he felt the power in the muscled body as Blackie slipped a large arm under his throat to apply a choke hold.

But that use of Blackledge's pure strength and not technique gave Merlin an opening. He was actually surprised when his mind had automatically whirled through his basic combat training and then the advanced martial arts techniques he had learned and a solution popped up. Wasn't survival instinct great?

Merlin turned his hip under the weight and threw a right elbow into a vulnerable spot...the big man's kidney.

Blackie grunted in pain and then tried to bring his arm tight around Merlin's neck again.

That brief moment gave Merlin another advantage and he twisted his body and drove a heavier blow to the kidneys.

Grunting in pain again, Blackie instinctively moved his own elbow down to protect his side.

Sliding out just enough to get leverage and the proper angle, Merlin drove an elbow into the big man's temple.

Stunned for just a moment, Blackie lessened his grip.

Scrambling around on his hands and knees, he then found the Beretta and spun around on his butt–

Blackie was already charging low across the few feet of concrete floor that separated them, his face a mask of rage as he slapped at the gun.

Merlin's knuckles felt like they were broken as the gun went flying. But he kept his wits about him and pushed his feet against the floor, driving himself backward.

Landing on the concrete instead of his opponent, Blackie growled in rage. He rose to his feet and dove after Merlin again.

But Merlin was still scooting away from his bigger opponent.

Blackie landed on his hands and knees this time. His muscles rippled as he rose and bellowed. "Fight, you coward."

But Merlin knew better and he continued pushing himself back, sliding his butt across the concrete floor. Another solution to his predicament came to him. He shook his head no, trying to put fear on his face. It this didn't work, he would probably be dead in the next few minutes.

Grinning maliciously, the big man took the bait. He rose to his feet, ran hard and launched himself at his smaller opponent.

Falling back and bringing his feet up, Merlin caught Blackie in the mid-section and used his weight against him, flipping him over.

Landing hard on his back, the big man's mouth opened in silent pain from the blow.

Merlin moved fast, swung around to his feet and behind a stack of boxes. He put his shoulder against the stack and grunted as he pushed hard.

Micah Blackledge's scream was cut off as he was buried under the heavy weight of the cardboard boxes containing four-pound jars of bullet casting flux.

Breathing heavy from the fast and furious exertion, Merlin was aware the gunfire outside the hut had ceased.

He had no time to lose.

Retrieving the Beretta and sticking it into the holster in the back of his jeans, Merlin moved across the floor and picked up one the wooden boxes containing a fifty-pound nuclear projectile. Setting it beside the back door, Merlin checked outside. The smoke was still heavy but everything was quiet. He pulled the Beretta and made his way back inside the Commando where he accessed the DAGR system. He searched the map for the shoot house that he had recorded on the flyover with the drone. He found it. He sent those coordinates to the cannon.

The cannon boomed and the Commando rocked. A moment later an explosion sounded in the distance.

Shouting sounded through the smoke and gunfire erupted again.

Where they were shooting, Merlin had no idea. He chose the obstacle training and assault course coordinates and fired again.

The vehicle rocked with the sound of the boom and an explosion sounded in the distance.

Next came the coordinates for the road leading into the compound and Merlin sent a 90mm shell in that direction. He was already out and running for the open door to the Quonset hut when it landed. That would confuse them to no ends as they wondered where the Commando was and what he would attack next. He worked as fast as possible, lugging the crates to the open door of the Commando and loading them inside. Once he was finished, he climbed inside the Commando, locked the side door and started the vehicle as he accessed the grenade launchers again. He had two choices; head back the way he came or take the shorter route through the rolling gates and the front door to the compound. He shot four smoke grenades up over the huts and then another four straight ahead. Which was where he decided to head. The diesel engine growled as he accelerated and shot along the back of the huts. Then he had another idea, one that should create more chaos and put a real crimp in the militia's activities. Taking a sharp turn to the left, Merlin took the vehicle one hundred yards away from the huts, rotated it around and set the coordinates for the last Quonset hut.

The Commando rocked as he fired and then an explosion was followed by a massive one as the ammunition inside the hut exploded right behind the 90mm shell.

Merlin ducked involuntarily, not only at the double explosion and the flash of light and flame but at the sounds of the bullets that ricocheted off the armor and the ballistic glass as the thousands and thousands of rounds remaining inside the hut went off from the heat of the fire.

Chapter 42

MERLIN ROTATED THE Commando in the direction of the rolling gate and took off at a 30 mph clip through the white rolling smoke. Ammunition was still going off but the rate was slowing. He accessed the machine gun and fired off to the right as he reached the far end of the huts, just to keep their heads down as he passed. But there was no return fire. He pushed the speed up to 40 mph, conscious of the fact he had taken out part of the road and he had no intention and falling into a crater and losing any advantage he had given himself.

But someone else wasn't as smart. A small car shot by on the road to the right, going twice as fast at least. It quickly disappeared into the smoke.

A few moments later, Merlin saw the quick flash of brake lights in the hazy smoke and then they disappeared. He slowed the Commando, watching for the crater. Sure enough he found the left edge of the hole he had blown almost dead center across the entrance road. Stopping the Commando, Merlin took the Beretta in hand and opened the side door. Since Blackie was more than likely still buried under a dozen heavy boxes and his men would no doubt stay to fight to the death, he assumed only one other person would be fleeing. And he wanted that one person if he was right. Climbing the soft edge of the crater, Merlin saw the back end of the small car through the blanket of smoke, nose down on the inside. He half-slid and half climbed down to the driver's door to see a swarthy man with a thick, black beard inside.

The man was holding the side of his head, where he appeared to have a lump, while frantically driving a shoulder against the door, trying to open it. The airbag had deployed and he had pushed it down to the dash but his door must have jammed when the front end slammed into the bottom of the hole.

Merlin flipped the Beretta around and smashed the glass in.

The man inside ducked away in surprise as the glass disintegrated in a shower of a thousand pieces. Then he looked at Merlin, wondering what was happening.

"Hello, Mr. Terrorist. Here, let me help you." Merlin grabbed the shoulder of his jacket and hauled him through the now-open window space.

"Hey. What are you doing–? Ow!"

"Sorry about that...*not*." As the man fell to the ground, Merlin flipped the Beretta around and pointed the business end at him, "If you resist, I'll shoot. Get it?"

"You can't do that. I have rights–"

Merlin slapped him across the face.

"Ow!"

"Listen, pal. I'm hungry, I'm tired and I'm cranky. I don't care about rights and stuff right now. So I repeat, Mr. Assaff. If you resist, I'll shoot you. Do you get it?"

A shocked look crossed his face at the fact Merlin knew his name and he nodded, "Yeah. I...."

"Good. Now climb up to the top of the crater."

Merlin followed a few feet to the side as the man climbed using his hands and feet. Once they were back on level ground, Merlin grabbed the man's sleeve and propelled him to the open door of the Commando, "Get in."

" I'm going. I'm going."

"Not fast enough." He pushed on the man's back as he climbed into the opening and he tumbled head over heels inside. Jumping in and pulling the door shut, Merlin gestured with the Beretta, "Move over there and lie face down, hands on your head." As the man complied in the tight quarters, Merlin got seated and drove for the rolling gate. The smoke dissipated as he reached the tree line and barreled for the gate. He took it at an angle and broke through, stopping just before the edge of the road. He made sure no innocents were going by and then he took off. Grabbing his cell phone, he thumbed a text message. As he did, he half-imagined the news story...man stopped by troopers while texting in an armored vehicle. He sent the message and went back to fully concentrating on his driving. Once he hit the main highway, he took the Commando up to top speed.

Ten minutes later, he heard a siren wailing from behind and closing fast.

Merlin wondered if a trooper was expecting him to pull over. Should he stop?

A moment later, a Georgia State Patrol car with lights flashing pulled into the passing lane and as it passed, Merlin saw the state trooper actually lean over to take a good look, the priceless look of amazement on his face. Then he simply shook his head and zoomed ahead to take up an escort position in front. Five minutes later, two more patrol cars joined the parade, escorting the Commando from behind. They kept the parade up all the way back to the U.S. Army

Reserve Armored Training Center. The road this time was blocked by troopers, though. But as his front escort peeled off and parked, one of the patrol cars sitting across the road pulled ahead and he was waved through.

There were at least a dozen other cars inside the blockade. He saw more Georgia State Patrol officers, several Gainesville PD and at least a dozen, dark vehicles with men in suits standing next to them. But there were only two men near his truck and Merlin was sure he recognized one of them. No, both of them. It was Detective Xavier Grummett and Detective Kaleb Jones. He parked dead center of the road, turned the Commando off, grabbed his cell phone and opened up the side door, "Okay, buddy. Let's go out and meet some friends."

The man on the floor complied but his face was long and his voice was angry as he got up, "You'll be hearing from my lawyer about this. I'll have your badge for this."

"If he can find me," Merlin said. "And who says I have a badge?"

The man did a double-take and then climbed out of the Commando, still grumbling about his rights as he stepped onto the pavement.

As Merlin stepped out behind him, Grummett and Jones approached.

Jones shook his head in amusement as he looked at the armored vehicle, "When you said it was better that we didn't know what you were going to do...."

Grummett nodded in agreement, "I'll say." Then he looked at the Beretta and the man with the heavy beard it was trained on, "This our friend out of New York?"

"Yeah. Meet Husain Assaff. He's your collar."

Jones's eyes lit up, "Yeah?" He stepped forward and turned the man around, "Hands behind your back double a and double f."

Assaff was surprised at the comment but he started complaining as he complied, "I have my rights. You have to read me my rights. That's what you have to do."

As the cuffs were slapped on the man, Merlin stuck the Beretta back into his holster, "That's what he kept telling me. But what do I know."

A grin split Grummett's face.

Jones took the man by the arm and turned him toward the dark cars and the men in suits, "Sorry, pal, but those guys will probably take you some place where rights don't exist."

Assaff continued complaining as Jones took him across the road but there was definite fear in his eyes.

Merlin gestured to the open door to the Commando, "The Atomic projectiles are in there. They're all yours, Detective Grummett."

"Seriously?"

"Yeah. The credit is all yours. It's the least I can do for shooting you."

Grummett put his hand out, "Thanks. Me and my partner never got your name."

Shaking his hand, Merlin said, "You know what they say. If I tell you that...."

Nodding in amusement, Grummett said, "Yeah, I know. Can we give you a ride somewhere?"

"No, thanks," Merlin said as he gestured to the pickup, "I have my own transportation." He clapped Grummett on the shoulder as he passed and headed for the driver side door. But just as he pulled the door open, he turned to Grummett and called out, "Actually, I just need to know one thing."

Chapter 43

MERLIN DROVE BACK to the airport in Atlanta, entering through gate number 19. As he had been told by the trooper originally, the guards at the gate never said a word. They just checked their computer system for his picture, had him place his hand on an iPad to get a scan of his hand and he was given a simple nod to pass.

The Bombardier Global 8000 was sitting on the tarmac in exactly the same spot. The airstairs were down and he wondered if they had always been that way while he was gone. Or if they had lowered it in readiness when he had texted Director Laurent what he'd done and that he was on his way back. It didn't really matter but the question reminded him this was all still new to him. Getting out of the pickup, he turned to the truck bed in back. Grabbing the case he had gotten from Grummett and Jones, he then headed for the airstairs.

Captain Charity Sherrell was in the doorway at the top. "Welcome back, sir," she called down. She moved back inside as Merlin climbed the stairs. "Are we heading home? We were told to expect you but...?"

"Yes, we're headed for home."

Captain Faith Saab stepped out from the back area, her hands combing her short blonde hair into place, "I'm all set."

Merlin set the case down on a seat and opened the top, pulling out a gallon jug with thick, black XXXs on the label, "This is for you two."

Sherrell's eyebrows knit together as she took the jug in hand.

A sheepish smile crossed Merlin's face, "Maybe you were just kidding but this is the famous Big Smoky Moonshine you asked for." That was what he had asked Detective Xavier Grummett about. Where to get the moonshine. Grummett and his partner Jones had been as happy as two kids when they personally led him to where he could find it.

Sherrell's eyes lit up when she looked in the box and saw the other three gallon jugs, "Well...I *was* just kidding. I never really thought you would do it...but...."

"But you'll take it?" Merlin asked.

Captain Faith Saab looked equally delighted, "Hell, yeah. If we weren't military, we'd kiss you. *Sir.*"

Merlin felt relieved, "Kisses are always welcome. But why don't we head for home? I'm tired."

The two officers immediately became officious and efficient. "Yes, sir," Sherrell said, "wheels up in five. We already have clearance."

Saab took the gallon jug from her fellow officer's hands and set it back inside the case, "I'll secure this with a seat belt and be right up. Don't want to damage our precious cargo, now do we?"

Merlin watched the two head off to their duties as he took the holster and gun and set it on one of the seats along with his cell phone. He settled into a comfy seat next to the window as he heard the airstairs close in place with a thick whump and the whine of the big engines start up. He looked out over the tarmac and that was the last thing he remembered.

SOMEONE WAS SHAKING him. "Sir?"

Merlin opened his eyes half way. He licked his lips and then looked to his right.

It was Captain Saab. "We've landed, sir."

Blinking his eyes and looking out the round window, Merlin saw they were pulled up to a large building, "We are? I don't even remember taking off...."

"No, sir. You fell asleep before I even got back to the flight cabin."

As Merlin rose, he heard the airstairs opening up and they were down on the tarmac and ready for him to descend by the time he stood in the doorway. The armored limousine was sitting twenty feet away, a soldier standing beside the open back door.

"We'll see you next time, sir."

Merlin turned and saw Captain Sherrell standing beside Saab. He wiped the sleep from his eyes as he gave them a nod, "Thanks for the ride, ladies. Don't drink all the moonshine at once."

"No, sir," Sherrell said, "we'll pace ourselves."

"Yeah. Two days at least," Saab added.

Merlin shot the two air officers a grin and then walked down the stairs to the tarmac and nodded at the soldier as he got into the armored limo.

Chapter 44

STONECLIFFE APARTMENTS

Ottawa, Canada

MERLIN KNOCKED SOFTLY on the door of the apartment down the hall from his own. He felt tired and wanted to sleep but was looking forward to seeing–

The door swung open and the luscious scent of a vanilla & dragon-fruit candle swirled in the air. The tall, willowy Jaimee Hartman appeared in a track suit, perspiration on her forehead, "Oh hi, Merlin. Me and Jigs were just doing our daily calisthenics."

"And just how much is Jigs doing?"

The thump, thump of cat paws sounded across the room inside the apartment and the blue, wooly Chartreux cat came running around the open door and leaped into Merlin's arms.

Merlin squeezed him, "Hey, pal. Did you miss me?"

Jaimee put on a pout and grumbled, "Hey, Jiggsy, you're making me feel like a third wheel. After all we've been through."

Putting his ear against the Chartreux's head, Merlin said, "What's that? You think I should take Miss Hartman out for a nice dinner to repay her? That sounds like a good idea."

Jaimee set her hands on her hips, "Oh. So now Jigs is trying to bribe my affections, is he?"

"He just thinks we should repay you–"

"And how do *you* plan on repaying me, Merlin Dragon?"

Merlin opened his mouth–

"Okay, okay. Lunch *and* a movie would be just great. And the National Arts Centre brought in the smash-hit musical Kinky Boots while you were gone." She held up two fingers, "And no being cheap. Two tickets, front row center."

"So it's dinner *and* a movie *and* the Arts Centre," Merlin repeated.

Jaimee raised an eyebrow, "You have a better idea?"

Merlin gave her a tired smile, "No. It's a deal." Then he squeezed Jigs again, "Now if you don't mind, I'm zonked. I haven't slept much in the last few days."

Jaimee shooed him away with her hand, "All right, go on you two."

As Merlin headed down the hall, he heard Jaimee call his name and he looked back.

She was holding on to the side of the door jamb and leaning out, "Keep in mind, I don't bite on the first date."

Merlin's eyebrows knit together.

"*But* the National Arts Centre will be a second date, so you never know."

Not sure what to say, and wondering if she was serious, Merlin just looked at her.

"And who knows what ideas the title Kinky Boots might cause."

Merlin was left standing in the hallway as Jaimee Hartman shut her door with a giggle. Rubbing the top of Jigs' head, he received a contented purr in return, "You know, Jigs...I've had an adventure I can tell you all about. What I can't tell you is how we deal with the women in our life. And how we take what they say as real or...."

The Chartreux gave him one of his brilliant smiles.

"Hey," Merlin complained. "Don't be so smug. I don't see you doing so well with that Siamese on the next balcony."

Also by Eugene Lloyd MacRae

A Rory Mack Steele Novel
Betrayal
Storm
Hunted
Stealing a Country
Fire Plague
Jewel
The Echelon Mind
The Chinese President
Knights of The Golden Circle
Cruise
Mask
The Overstolz Code
Box Set: Rory Mack Steele Thrillers Books 1-12

The Stopper Files
Iron Pipeline
Economic Hitman

Whiskey Empire
King of the Bootleggers
Gangsters
'Ndrangheta
Vendetta
Burn Powder
King of the Bootleggers Box Set

Watch for more at eugenelloydmacrae.com.